His fiery kiss
still stung Kylie's lips

"All you want is to satisfy your uncontrolled libido!" she cried.

"Hardly uncontrolled, sweetheart." Race glanced mockingly at his bandaged arm. "My injuries prevent anything more... strenuous."

"Three cheers for small mercies!" she flung back. "Maybe every cloud *does* have a silver lining."

Race rose leisurely to his feet. "Not yours. You've made all the money you're going to out of my uncle. The next time he goes touring you won't be with him."

"And just how do you propose to stop me?" Kylie scoffed.

His taunting smile sent prickles down her spine. "You'll find out when the time comes, tiger eyes. Just remember that I'm awake to your little caper. And to your...shall we say...vulnerable points?"

Mixed Feelings

by

KERRY ALLYNE

Harlequin Books

TORONTO • LONDON • LOS ANGELES • AMSTERDAM
SYDNEY • HAMBURG • PARIS • STOCKHOLM • ATHENS • TOKYO

Original hardcover edition published in 1981
by Mills & Boon Limited

ISBN 0-373-02479-7

Harlequin edition published June 1982

Printed in U.S.A.

CHAPTER ONE

As soon as Kylie's introduction to Grant Brandon's surprisingly young housekeeper had been completed, the trim blonde-haired woman turned back to their joint employer with her brows arching expressively.

'You certainly made excellent time in getting back here,' she applauded.

'Thanks to Kylie,' Grant smiled down at the girl beside him.

Kylie gave a self-deprecating smile in response but didn't comment. After all, her driving ability had been one of the reasons for her having been hired. Up until two months ago she had been working at a service station on Queensland's Gold Coast, and when she wasn't dispensing the motorists' usual needs of petrol and oil, it had been her job to test-drive the vehicles once the mechanics had finished working on them in the repair bays.

That was also where she had met Grant Brandon. The tall, spare-framed, kindly-looking retired grazier from near Broken Hill in far western New South Wales had been a regular customer during his stay with friends at Paradise Waters, and because of his friendly, courteous manner he had rapidly become one of her favourites. She had known from their casual talks that he was finding the long distances to be travelled on his long-promised tour around Australia to see new sights and renew old acquaintances somewhat lonely—as well as causing some discomfort while he was driving, owing to

5

the arthritic condition in his knees—but it had still come as a complete shock when he had suddenly offered her the position as his chauffeuse/companion.

Initially, she had been extremely doubtful of accepting, even though it was a unique opportunity for her to see so much of the country. She really didn't know him all that well, and the idea of roaming over vast tracts of isolated territory in company with a virtual stranger had, to say the least, made her a little apprehensive. Her parents had been flatly against the proposal until they had met Grant themselves a few times, whereupon they had gradually begun to change their minds—he had a charmingly persuasive manner—and in the end had willingly approved of her eventual decision to accept the post.

During the last six weeks the two of them had been slowly making their way north along the beautiful eastern coastline before planning to head inland. However, when some friends of Grant's on a cattle stud outside Rockhampton had informed him that they had heard, via the bush telegraph, that his nephew—who was running his uncle's adjoining sheep station together with his own—had suffered some sort of accident, those plans had altered dramatically. A telegram to Grant's property had elicited the information that a collarbone, an arm, and three ribs had been broken as a result of the mishap and, despite the allegations they received in return that everything was under control, they had returned to Wanbanalong post haste.

'And it happened while they were mustering, did it?' Grant continued in a sober tone as they headed across the verandah to the screen door leading into the homestead.

'Mmm, out in the Ridge Paddock,' Abby Lucas replied. 'His horse came down and rolled on him.'

A heavy frown descended on to her employer's forehead. 'About two or three weeks ago, I think he said in his telegram?'

'That's right,' she nodded.

Grant stepped back to allow the two women to enter the house first. 'You should have got in touch with me straight away, instead of letting me hear about it by chance,' he reproved.

'I would have done, if it had been left to me,' the wry return came quickly. 'But someone else had different ideas on the matter.'

'Stubborn, independent fool!' he snorted, but more in grudging admiration than in disparagement. 'Where is he, anyway? Over at Elouera Springs?'

'No, he's here.' Suddenly Abby began to laugh. 'In fact, I'm surprised he hasn't come storming out here to find what's been keeping me. I was on my way to make some coffee when I heard your vehicle pull up. I'm afraid being confined to the homestead for so long hasn't exactly been to his liking.'

'I can imagine,' he averred drily. 'But if you're making coffee, make it for all of us, would you, please, Abby? We'll have it in the office. I presume that is where we'll find him?' His accompanying glance was enquiringly made.

'That's where,' she confirmed expressively before continuing on her way down the hall.

Grant looked at Kylie and his blue eyes twinkled. 'Feel like bearding a frustrated lion in his den?' he asked whimsically.

'I'm game if you are,' she grinned, showing perfectly

even teeth in a gleaming white smile, and followed him through a comfortably furnished sitting room to another room beyond. 'It does sound as if he took a nasty fall, though.'

'But the breaks were all clean ones, that's the main thing,' he returned more seriously. 'And at thirty-four he's still young and healthy enough for them to heal without too much trouble.'

'It's just the waiting that's the problem!'

'Something like that,' he laughed, and led her into a partially glass-enclosed office at the side of the house.

Their approaching voices had obviously alerted the man sitting at the desk inside, for his eyes were fastened expectantly on the doorway when they entered. And what fabulous eyes they were, noted Kylie after only a moment's inspection. The clearest green she had ever beheld and framed by the thickest and longest black lashes she had ever known a man to possess. The rest of his features weren't exactly repulsive either, she was to decide ruefully a short second later. His hair was as dark as night and slightly curling above a strong, good-looking face which owned a firm curving mouth and a bold, determined jaw. His polished bronze skin denoted long hours spent in the open air in all kinds of weather, and certainly hadn't been acquired as a social tan.

'Grant!' he exclaimed in a mixture of pleasure and wry amusement at the sight of his relative as he rose carefully to his feet and extended his left hand. His right one was encased in plaster back to his elbow and supported in a sling. 'It's good to see you! Although, as I said in my telegram, there really wasn't any need for you to interrupt your trip.'

Their hands met in a firm clasp even as Grant retorted in a dry tone, 'No, it doesn't look like it.'

'Oh, these.' An oblique grin crooked the younger
man's mouth as he glanced down at his various dressings. 'They're restricting, but I'm still managing.'

'No doubt! But at what cost to your rate of re-
covery?'

'None whatsoever if you disregard the frustration,'
his nephew laughed with implicit feeling. 'But had I
known you intended bringing such an attractive visitor
with you,' emerald green eyes subjected Kylie to a lazy,
but extremely comprehensive, appraisal, 'I may have
had second thoughts about the matter.'

'Is that so?' Grant's lips pursed humorously. With
her own suntanned cheeks staining with unexpected
colour Kylie dropped her tawny-eyed gaze to the clut-
tered desk which separated her from the tall figure on
the other side. 'Well, for your information,' his uncle
went on in the same amused voice, 'Kylie isn't really a
visitor, as such, at all. She happens to be my driver/
companion who I mentioned in my message.'

'But whose sex you—er—inadvertently forgot to dis-
close.'

A slightly mocking inflection in the voice had Kylie
raising her eyes again, but only to find herself receiving
another bright-eyed assessment. A somewhat less appreciative one this time, however, it seemed.

'I thought I'd surprise you,' chuckled Grant.

'Oh, you've certainly done that!' The concession was
made in eloquent tones.

'I thought as much,' Grant laughed again. 'But now I
suppose an introduction is due, so . . .' he turned to the
girl next to him, 'Kylie, allow me to present my repro-

bate nephew, Race Brandon. Kylie Townsend.'

'How do you do?' she began diffidently. There was something about this man that was making her horribly selfconscious. Then, realising it wasn't the most appropriate greeting she could have offered under the circumstances, she embarrassedly tried to amend it. 'I'm sorry, I just didn't think,' she half smiled. 'I guess it would have been more tactful if I'd said I'm pleased to meet you.'

A heavily muscled shoulder was hunched unconcernedly. 'Think nothing of it,' he discounted easily, and held out a hand towards her. 'I'm glad to meet you too, Kylie, and to see how well you're obviously taking care of Grant's creature comforts. He looks a new man since I saw him last.'

Was he by any chance implying what she suspected he was implying? That it wasn't an altogether platonic relationship she was sharing with his uncle? At the idea that he might be, resentment abruptly obliterated Kylie's previous discomfiture at the unfounded insinuation. Since she had taken the position with Grant it wasn't the first time that the notion of a twenty-one-year-old girl becoming the companion of a man three times her age had raised some suspicious eyebrows along their route—as well as drawing some snide remarks—but she definitely hadn't expected to receive them in her employer's own home! Her gaze was defiant now when it connected with the man before her and she took his outstretched hand with deliberate positiveness.

'How kind of you to say so,' she made herself smile provokingly.

The pressure from the work-hardened fingers grasping hers tightened perceptively, almost painfully, but it was worth it from Kylie's point of view and she refused to give him the satisfaction of having her break contact prematurely because of it. Instead, she took her time, and when she finally withdrew her hand there was a tiny smile of triumph catching at the soft sweep of her lips. She had no intention of allowing this somewhat overwhelming nephew of her employer to put her on the defensive.

'My word, she's looking after me well,' Grant now endorsed with a fond smile as he rested a hand on her shoulder, and apparently oblivious to the undercurrent in their words. 'I couldn't have made a better choice if I'd tried. Not only is she a competent and reliable driver, but she's also an appreciative and rejuvenating companion as well.'

'Oh, I wouldn't doubt that for a minute.' Race's firm mouth quirked mockingly.

'But to get back to you . . .' His uncle's thoughts returned to the reason for them being there, holding out a chair for Kylie, then taking one himself as Race resumed his own seat. 'How *are* your injuries progressing?'

'Mending well, by all accounts. If it wasn't for this—' the younger man patted the strapping beneath his denim shirt which was giving him a barrel-chested appearance. Not that Kylie thought he would look much smaller without the padding, because he was certainly a powerfully built character. '—I could probably give riding a try. But as it is, I can't ride or drive.' His expression was one of disgust at his own immobility.

'You could always get one of the men to drive you if it was absolutely necessary,' Grant proposed, but it only drew a negating shake of the head from his nephew.

'Not at the moment, we're already short-handed, what with the shearing muster and all.'

'What about Abby, then?'

'Mmm, what about me?' asked the housekeeper curiously, entering the room with a loaded tray which she proceeded to place on the desk.

'He was just suggesting you may have been able to drive me around while I'm incapacitated,' Race relayed with an unexpected grin.

'Oh?' Abby couldn't keep the laughter out of her voice while she poured out the steaming coffee and handed round the cups. 'You must have done something to upset him if he's wishing that on you.'

The enigmatic interplay brought an uncomprehending frown to Kylie's forehead, and Grant didn't look much wiser either, as evidenced by his rather confused, 'And what, may I ask, is that supposed to mean?'

'Only that it must be quite some time since you last saw me drive,' laughed Abby, making for the door. 'I'm afraid I haven't improved much over the years and you're still liable to be thrown through the windscreen whenever I change gears. If it's not an automatic, a leaping kangaroo has nothing on me when I get behind the wheel!'

Grant's expression was rueful as he returned his attention to his nephew once Abby had departed. 'You mean she's still no better than she ever was?'

' 'Fraid not,' Race drawled wryly.

'In that case, there's only one thing for it,' Grant sighed, and gave Kylie an encouraging smile. A smile, however, which had her replacing the cup she had been about to drink from on its matching saucer with a clatter, and staring back at him in something very close to dismay. Oh, no, he couldn't! 'I guess I'll just have to loan you Kylie for the time being.'

Oh, yes, he could! she grimaced inwardly in despair.

'And postpone the rest of your trip? As I said before, there's really no need.'

Kylie held her breath. Perhaps there was hope yet.

'That's a matter of opinion,' retorted Grant gruffly. 'Naturally we'll stay until you've fully recovered, and I'm sure Kylie will be only too glad to help you in any way she can. We both will, won't we, lass?'

What could she say? It was the last thing she wanted, but, for Grant's sake, she managed a convincingly co-operative, 'Of course.'

'You're sure you can spare her?'

Race's tone was so sardonic and, to Kylie's ears, there was such a wealth of meaning in his words that she swung her gaze to her employer in anticipation. Surely he must realise what his nephew was implying now!

But Grant's response showed nothing of the kind. He merely replied in all seriousness, 'Oh, I think so. Besides, now that we're not travelling I wouldn't want her to become bored being tied to an old coot like me all day.'

'As if I would!' Kylie protested immediately, vehemently. 'And you're not an old coot either! You're a very charming and intelligent gentleman, and I thoroughly enjoy the time I spend in your company.' And Race Brandon could make of that whatever he damned well pleased!

Grant laughed delightedly and flicked a teasing glance across the desk. 'Now you see what I meant when I said I couldn't have made a better choice,' he crowed.

'I do indeed,' acceded Race ironically, and not a little caustically. He raised his cup and fixed Kylie with a taunting look of derision over its rim. 'I can see it's going to be quite an experience having someone of such intense loyalty and—um—dedication around.'

Kylie pressed her lips together vexedly at the subtle gibe and lowered her dark curling lashes, but not so far that she couldn't continue to covertly, direfully, study her cynical antagonist. So he thought it was going to be quite an experience, did he? Well, he didn't know the half of it, yet, she smiled to herself pleasurably. If he chose to believe there was more to her relationship with his uncle than there actually was, then she certainly wasn't going to be the one to disillusion him. In fact, it might even prove amusing to further his assumption. When the truth came out he would be the one feeling discomfited, and surely she was entitled to some recompense for his odious suppositions.

Naturally enough, the men's conversation began to veer towards matters concerning the property and the happenings which had occurred since Grant departed on his tour some months previously, so Kylie took the opportunity to survey her surroundings a little more closely. From what she had seen so far the homestead appeared to be an old but well cared for house with large rooms—at least the sitting room had been—wherein a variety of modernising renovations had been carried out at intervals down through the years.

Even the office was of a size to accommodate all three of them quite easily without seeming crowded, and it contained a typical range of business equipment.

The walls were painted a cool and restful pale green, the timberwork a highly polished oak, while the carpet covering the floor was of a hard-wearing variety necessary to withstand the heavy tread of riding boots and work shoes. The outside wall was glass from ceiling to waist height, and it was here that her gaze lingered the longest. The sheet immensity of the panorama beyond those panes of glass fascinated her.

She had lived all her life on the Gold Coast with its high-rise resort hotels and apartments, bustling holiday crowds filling the streets and long golden beaches, and where it was necessary to stare out to sea if one wanted an uninterrupted view for more than fifty metres. But here she could allow her eyes to wander unhindered across flatter land than she could ever have imagined until it merged with a faded blue sky, and there wasn't a single thing higher than a stunted shrub to block the view. She was well aware, of course, that it wasn't the same in every direction around the homestead, because they had followed a line of low hump-backed hills and tree-lined creek beds when they had driven on to the property earlier that afternoon, but this scene from the office was the one which intrigued her the most. It had a mesmerising quality which made her keep scanning the distance, as if in an effort to prove her eyesight wrong by finding a building, or a person, or something out there other than miles upon miles of sun-scorched emptiness.

So captivated was she with her private musings that it wasn't until she heard Grant laugh and he touched her on the arm that Kylie realised he had concluded his conversation with his nephew and was preparing to leave.

'What's caught your interest so strongly, little one?' His kindly blue eyes roamed over her pensive features curiously, humorously.

'Nothing,' she tilted her head back to smile up at him. 'But that's just it. I keep thinking there has to be something other than unlimited space out there. It's all so very different from what I'm used to.'

'Disappointingly different, I'm sure, to one used to discos and nightclubs on every second corner,' put in Race, a quiet contempt uppermost.

'Not at all,' she denied quickly, and sent him a taunting smile. 'I'd be more inclined to call it satisfyingly different, as a matter of fact.'

'Of course she would,' Grant certified confidently. 'Kylie isn't the type to worry over a little isolation, otherwise she wouldn't have signed on to come touring with me to some of the remote places I intend visiting.'

A sceptical smile caught at Race's mouth. 'Ah, yes, I was forgetting, it was purely a desire to travel that brought you two together, wasn't it?'

Rising leisurely to her feet, Kylie swept her shoulder-length rich brown hair back from her cheeks, her sidelong glance purposely goading. 'There were other considerations,' she purred with insinuating emphasis. 'Your uncle is a very considerate and rewarding person to be with.'

The barb obviously reached its mark, because Race promptly came out of his chair in a far more hurried fashion than Kylie had hers. But as he did so a grimace of pain chased its way across his face, and a stifled oath left his lips as he clapped a broad hand to his bound ribs.

Grant took an immediate step forward. 'Are you all

right?' he inquired worriedly.

'Yes, you really ought to be more careful,' added
Kylie, but with rather more doubtful concern. Although, if the truth were known, she did indeed feel a
twinge of guilt at having been the cause of him forgetting his injuries. She only wanted to needle the man, not
to cripple him. 'Why didn't you say you needed a hand
up? I would have helped you,' she offered facetiously.

'You're too kind,' Race drawled in the same tongue-
in-cheek manner. 'But I don't happen to be a *complete*
invalid, thanks all the same. I can still manage to do
some things for myself.'

'Mmm, so I saw,' she couldn't resist mocking.

He rested one square, workmanlike hand on a lean
hip and laughed sardonically. 'A once only, I can assure
you, and only because I was unprepared. It won't
happen again,' he predicted decisively.

'I should hope not,' Grant returned to the conversation brusquely, 'or you're likely to find yourself back in
hospital before you know it.'

'But not today. Not while I have so much paperwork
to keep me safely tied to this chair for the rest of the
afternoon,' Race asserted with a dry smile pulling at his
lips as he sank slowly back into his seat. He aimed a
lazily hopeful glance in Kylie's direction. 'You don't
happen to have had any secretarial experience, I suppose?'

A responsive grin appeared before she could forestall
it, but she shook her head. 'Sorry, office work has never
been in my line. I like the open air too much.'

'After two weeks inside, I'd have thought you would
have it all up to date by now,' surmised Grant in surprise.

'It is for this place, but these,' Race indicated the books and papers laying before him, 'are for Elouera Springs. They've been mounting steadily in my absence and Adrian brought them over this morning.'

His uncle nodded comprehendingly. 'Well, I guess we'd better leave you to it, then.' His expression turned rueful as he looked at Kylie. 'We still have to unpack before dinner.'

'Never mind, I'll do yours for you,' she offered promptly, and began moving towards the open doorway.

'Oh, by the way,' Race called before they left, 'Selena and Victor are coming for dinner this evening. They said they'd be here about seven.'

'That's good,' Grant acknowledged equably. 'It will give Kylie a chance to meet some of our neighbours.'

'Do they live very far from here?' asked Kylie interestedly once they had resumed walking.

'Not very. About fifteen miles, that's all. Their property adjoins Wanbanalong on its eastern boundary.'

'While Race is your neighbour to the north, I think you once said?'

'That's right. He took over Elouera Springs when his father—my brother Jeff—died.'

'I see,' she murmured thoughtfully. 'So who's running his property while he's here? His mother?' She paused and then determinedly added, 'His wife?'

Grant gave a not altogether amused laugh. 'No, to both suggestions. One, he hasn't got a wife, and two,' his voice hardened noticeably, 'his mother cleared off with another man when he was five years old and hasn't been heard from since.'

A deep frown furrowed Kylie's forehead. 'You mean

she just vanished into thin air? She never wrote, or even tried to get in touch . . . with her son, at least?'

'No, she left a half-page note the day she departed, but since that time the only news we've had of her has been of an indirect nature.' His mouth firmed to an unyielding line. 'Fay was never the maternal type. After Race was born she refused to have any more children in case it ruined her figure. She was always more concerned for her looks than she was for her child.'

They passed out of the sitting room and into the hall without either of them really being aware of it, Kylie's thoughts returning to the man they had just left. From his self-assured manner it was almost impossible to believe he had received such a distressing setback so early in his life.

'At least he's fortunate in that it doesn't seem to have left any lasting scars,' she mused out loud.

'Oh, no?' It wasn't a question so much as a contradiction.

'Well, it certainly didn't make him lose any confidence in himself,' she just had to point out, a trifle acidly.

'Not in himself, no, thank God!' Grant confirmed expressively. 'But where women are concerned, that's another matter. As you were quick to notice.'

'I was?' Golden-brown eyes widened in astonishment.

'You were,' he reiterated drily. 'Or did you think I was too senile to realise there was a verbal battle going on between the pair of you?'

As they both knew she didn't consider him senile she didn't bother to refute that point, but went on immediately to probe, 'You mean, you knew all along that he suspects I'm—er . . .' she flushed and cleared her throat selfconsciously, 'a more familiar kind of companion than I actually am?'

The corners of his mouth pulled in sharply as he nodded. 'I did.'

'Then why didn't you say something?' she queried confusedly. 'Tell him how wrong he was?'

Stopping at a door leading from the hallway, he opened it but didn't immediately enter the room beyond. 'There didn't seem much point while you were doing everything you could to convince him he was correct,' he returned with a sigh. 'I thought my best course was to ignore the pair of you and continue as if nothing was wrong.'

For the first time since she had known him he sounded disappointed in her and Kylie followed him into the room with a downcast look on her face. 'I'm sorry, Grant,' she apologised wistfully. 'Are you very annoyed with me?'

In response he lifted a gnarled weatherbeaten hand and ran it fondly over her shining hair. 'Not annoyed, lass, so much as concerned,' he replied heavily. 'You see, the man who bought his mother—and I mean that almost literally—was old enough to be her father, and if you give Race enough reason to see a parallel between her case and yours, then I'm afraid all hell could break loose round here very shortly ... with you the chief target!'

'Oh, lord, I've really started something, haven't I?' she grimaced ruefully.

'Mmm, that you have,' he half smiled. 'And I'm very curious to know why.' His gaze held hers expectantly.

Kylie shifted from one foot to the other and hunched a slender shoulder defensively. 'I—I figured it would serve him right if I did string him along a bit, then maybe another time he wouldn't be so ready to jump to conclusions,' she admitted with a trace of defiance in her tone.

'And now?'

She took a deep breath and said exactly what was on her mind. 'I still think he needs to be taught a lesson! He had no right to imply what he did!'

'Meaning, you intend to continue deliberately giving him the wrong impression?'

'I—well—no, not exactly, I guess. Not if you don't want me to.' Her tawny eyes darkened with a plea for understanding. 'But I can't go, cap in hand, begging forgiveness for having misled him either! I'm sorry, but I just can't!'

'Did I ask you to?'

'No, but . . .'

'But what?'

'Isn't that the only move that's likely to convince him it's all been an unfortunate misunderstanding?' she queried, sardonically flippant.

'Not really,' he frowned. 'I could explain to him that . . .'

'No!' she broke in quickly, and surprising even herself with the vehemence with which she said it. 'Please—I don't want you making excuses for me. It would be too embarrassing, and—and . . .'

'What's wrong, Kylie?' Grant turned her troubled face up to his with a gentle hand. 'There's more to this than you're telling me, isn't there?'

Like suddenly discovering she was undeniably attracted to someone who obviously wasn't about to return the feeling? her mind suggested insidiously.

'Of course not!' she disclaimed hastily, to quell her own dismaying thoughts as much as to answer him. 'What else could there be?'

'That's what I'd like to find out,' he half laughed ruefully, releasing her. 'But whether a lesson is needed or not, I think something's going to have to be said before too much longer. There could be some very disturbing consequences—for all concerned—otherwise.'

Kylie nodded slowly, regretfully. 'I'm sorry, I didn't think, but I guess I've made the situation pretty embarrassing for you as well, haven't I?'

Grant's blue eyes twinkled unexpectedly. 'In my case, flattering would be a more apt description, I believe,' he chuckled. Then, as an answering smile began to shape her lips, he changed the subject by sweeping an arm wide to encompass the bedroom which was obviously meant to be hers during her stay, asking, 'What do you think?'

She hadn't taken much notice since following him inside, but now she really took note of the simply but fashionably furnished room and promptly nodded her approval.

'It's lovely, thank you, and I'm sure I'm going to enjoy my stay here. That is, provided . . .' She halted, her thoughts resolutely remaining with their previous conservation, her smile gradually fading. 'I don't really have any choice but to try and make amends with your nephew, do I?' she sighed.

'I'm afraid not, if you won't let me do it for you,' he agreed in a commiserating fashion.

With a grimace Kylie pushed her hands deep into the back pockets of her jeans and paced towards the window where she stood for a moment before swinging back to face him tautly.

'All right, I'll try,' she promised grudgingly. A spark of apologetic defiance flashed momentarily in her eyes. 'But he'd better be prepared to believe me, because I don't intend pleading with him! It is his fault, after all! If he hadn't been so anxious to think the worst, none of this would have happened.'

'And if someone else hadn't been quite so quick to give credence to his misconception, then maybe none of this would be necessary either,' he countered drily.

A rueful grin turned up the edges of her mouth. 'Okay, I admit I'm not exactly blameless, but more importantly . . . is your nephew about to be as strictly truthful in conceding that it was his suspicious mind that created all this ferment in the first place?' she quizzed in ironic tones.

CHAPTER TWO

KYLIE was to receive an answer to her question sooner than she anticipated, for when she left Grant's room after doing his unpacking for him, she almost collided with Race as he was passing the door and, deciding she probably wouldn't get a better opportunity, she looked up at him enquiringly.

'May I have a word with you, please?'

Briefly, his eyes flicked towards the door she had just closed behind her. 'Are you sure you've got the time?' he drawled sarcastically.

It was an effort for Kylie not to spin on her heel and walk away, right then and there, but for her employer's sake she gritted her teeth and remained where she was.

'Yes, I have the time,' she replied with controlled fierceness. 'Do you?'

'That depends.' He began walking again and she had, perforce, to do likewise.

'On what?'

'On how long it's likely to take. I'm afraid washing and dressing for dinner is a somewhat lengthy process for me these days,' he explained, eyeing his injuries significantly.

'Then I won't stop you.' She eagerly took a step away from him.

Before she could take another one, however, Race had snapped out his left arm with incredible swiftness to imprison one of her wrists within a steely grasp. 'I'll be the one to decide whether I have the time or not,' he advised mockingly. 'So suppose you just tell me what all this is about, eh?'

After a few seconds spent unsuccessfully trying to free herself, Kylie had to be content with glaring at him resentfully. 'It's about all the totally unwarranted and extremely offensive inferences you keep making!' she fired hotly, and not at all in the rational manner she had intended to use.

Race inclined his head to one side quizzically. 'My *what*?' he laughed in outright amusement.

'Your baseless insinuations regarding Grant and myself!' she clarified stormily, and struggling not only for freedom now, but for equilibrium as well. He was too disastrously attractive for her to concentrate when he laughed like that.

'Baseless?' The laugh which issued from his bronzed throat this time definitely wasn't amused. 'I'd like to know how they were baseless when you were so keen to confirm them! Perhaps you'd care to enlighten me while I'm getting ready for dinner,' he suggested satirically, throwing open another door and pulling her into the room after him. His lip curled hatefully as he slammed the door shut again with the side of his foot. 'I don't doubt you're no stranger to a man's bedroom.'

'How dare you!' Kylie lashed out furiously at his goading face with her free hand, but only to have it miss completely when he jerked back out of reach. Then, in a rapid switch she was unable to forestall, she found she was the one under attack when he wrapped his fingers within her hair, holding her head captive, and his face lowered disturbingly near.

'You can count yourself lucky I didn't automatically

block that swing of yours with this,' he advised roughly, and nodding to the plastered arm which separated them. 'Otherwise you could have joined me with a broken bone or two of your own.'

'In that case, I'm surprised you didn't use it deliberately,' she retorted bitterly.

'Are you?' Green eyes clashed perturbingly with tawny gold.

Kylie swallowed convulsively. She felt as if she was drowning in an emerald sea. There wasn't so much as a single fleck of another hue to mar the purity of colour in those dusky-framed eyes gazing into hers. Her lips were suddenly dry too and, without even being aware of it, she slid the tip of her tongue swiftly over them. The action at least served to divert Race's attention, but so devastatingly that her brief moment of relief barely had time to register.

'Oh, what the hell!' he muttered savagely, forcing her mouth up to his. 'Grant's too old for you, anyhow!'

With a smothered sound of protest Kylie tried to drag her head from his grip, but it was useless. He had too firm a hold, and his lips went right on demanding a response she was all too frightened she might give. Her hands came up intent on pummelling her way free, but encountering the cast on his arm and feeling the heavy strapping about his chest, they remained clenched, but still, where they lay. Not even to escape the increasing pressure which was forcing her lips apart, and robbing her of coherent thought, could she purposely take the chance on causing him added injury.

When at last he put her from him she knew it was only because he had finally succeeded in gaining what he wanted—her unmistakable surrender—and tears of dismay started to her eyes, spiking her lashes.

'You're despicable!' she choked scathingly, wrapping her arms about her midriff.

'Because I kissed you . . . or because I elicited a response?'

A humiliating warmth crept into Kylie's cheeks, but she held his sardonic gaze valiantly. 'Because I came in here to talk to you, not to be insulted and treated like some cheap tramp!' she railed, and began storming for the door.

'Not yet, tiger eyes.' Race had hold of the handle to prevent her leaving before she was aware of him moving. 'We haven't even started our discussion yet, let alone finished it.'

The lazily drawled nickname threw her off balance for a moment, making her glance waver uncertainly and then fall. 'There's no reason to begin. I already know what the result will be.' Raising her head again, she sent him a gibing look. 'I can see now that getting you to change your mind would be on a par with reversing the tide . . . impossible!'

'Is that so?' Leaning back against the door, he proceeded to leisurely unbutton his shirt. 'Well, suppose you try, just for the fun of it, eh?'

'Fun?' she repeated in disbelief. 'I can assure you I find nothing at all humorous in any of this. And—and would you mind not undressing in front of me!' she ordered indignantly. Now that he had removed the sling from around his neck Race was shrugging out of his shirt altogether.

'Don't tell me you're embarrassed?' One dark eyebrow arched ironically as he eased the rolled sleeve over the cast and tossed the denim garment on to the end of the bed.

'Yes, I am, as a matter of fact!'

'You surprise me,' drily. 'I would have thought you'd be used to half-naked bodies after living at a beach resort like the Gold Coast.'

'It isn't the same,' she murmured awkwardly. And it definitely wasn't in this instance, for although a large part of his torso was covered with a dressing, there was still enough bare skin visible to make her disconcertingly aware of him in a strictly physical sense, and the knowledge had her shuffling uncomfortably from one foot to the other. 'So, if you'll please move out of the way, I'll be leaving now,' she concluded in the same diffident whisper.

Race stepped away from the door, but not to enable her to make an exit. Instead, he uttered a vetoing, 'Uh-uh!' and, catching hold of her upper arm, steered her across to the bed where she was pressed, regardless of her objections, into sitting on its edge. 'We still have to talk, remember?' he taunted. 'Besides, you can make yourself useful by re-fastening this strapping,' he pulled at an end which had worked itself loose, 'and helping me dress. You did say in the office that you were willing to do *anything* you could to help, didn't you?' He sent her an infuriating look of aggravation.

'But that didn't include acting as your nurse or your valet!' she hurled back at him, and bouncing angrily to her feet.

'Are you refusing?'

The question was put so quietly, so watchfully, that Kylie was instantly on her guard. Was he hoping she would, just to give him an opportunity to cause trouble for her with Grant? She could well believe him capable of it, and of presenting her in the worst possible light as he did so!

'No, I'm not refusing,' she smouldered resentfully at having to back down. It certainly went against the grain where this man was involved. 'But only out of regard for Grant, not for any other reason!'

'Ah, yes, Grant!' He retrieved a roll of adhesive plaster and a pair of scissors from the chest of drawers beside him and handed them to her with a derisive glint in his eyes. 'You were going to explain to me something about the relationship you've managed to create for yourself with him, I believe?'

Kylie peeled off a strip of the tape and cut through it with a vicious snap of the scissors. 'For a start, I haven't *created* any sort of relationship with him, and certainly not of the type that you're trying to infer!' she informed him hotly. Slapping the cut tape into his hand for him to hold, she returned the rest to the chest of drawers, then set to work tightening the bandaging about his chest with as much composure as she could muster.

'And just what type is that?' he asked in feigned ignorance.

'That he—that we—that I'm . . .'

She couldn't bring herself to say it, but Race had no such qualms, and his voice was glacially cold as he denounced contemptuously, 'That you're sleeping with him! That you're using that lovely face and temptingly endowed body of yours in order to gain remunerations you wouldn't otherwise be receiving! Is that what you were trying to say?'

'No! Because it just isn't true!' she cried desperately, the tail of the bandage dropping from her shaking fingers. Oh, God, how could she have been so stupid as to actively encourage him in thinking such things?

'It was true this afternoon ... by your own admittance!'

'But I only said those things because you made me annoyed with your first insinuation!'

Race gave a short bark of laughter totally devoid of humour. 'You'll have to do better than that, sweetheart,' he jeered. 'I think you'll find denial is the accepted form of dissent in such cases, not furtherance!'

'It's also the accepted form to give someone the benefit of the doubt before condemning them out of hand!' She tried a little attacking herself.

'Of course! If there *is* any doubt,' he countered arrogantly.

'Oh, I see,' she fumed, her breasts rising and falling rapidly due to her increased rate of breathing. 'Young girl, older man, and as far as you're concerned there's only one possible conclusion to be drawn, is that it? Well, now I'll tell you something, Race Brandon,' she went on in the same incensed manner without giving him a chance to reply. 'For your information, all women don't happen to be made in the same mould as your mother, and ...' With a horrified gasp she came to a halt, her eyes widening in dismay. In her anger she was saying things she hadn't meant to mention at all.

Race's shapely mouth thinned to an inflexible line. 'You were saying ...?' he prompted menacingly.

Kylie put out a placatory hand, then just as swiftly withdrew it. 'I'm sorry—I didn't mean ... oh, damn, that bandage is unravelling,' she stammered confusedly. At the moment her thoughts were too haphazard for her to present them in any semblance of order.

'Forget the bandage!' he grated, and flung the tape he was holding on to the bed.

'But you can't let it come undone!' She rushed forward to pick it up again. Not only was she worried about what the result would be if he did lose the support of the dressing, but she also considered it a slightly safer subject to concentrate on right now. 'Here, let me tighten it again.'

'I said . . . forget it!' His left hand snaked out to grip her wrist painfully when she made to take hold of the bandage. 'I'm still waiting to hear what connection my mother has with you and Grant.'

'Wh-when I've f-finished this,' she defied intrepidly, albeit not very forcefully. 'It's more important.'

Moments passed during which she thought he wasn't going to comply, but to her relief, his grasp finally began to relax and she heard him utter a resigned sigh.

'You're suddenly taking the nursing bit to heart, aren't you?' he gibed wryly.

'It's obvious someone needs to,' she shrugged, and moved around to his back in order to make certain she didn't leave any slack. 'You seem more intent on putting yourself back into hospital than in getting better.'

'And who's been the cause of that, I wonder?'

While she was behind him Kylie could afford to let a tiny smile curve the soft contours of her mouth. 'Perhaps you shouldn't be so ready to believe the worst of people,' she ventured in a murmur.

'Not people, sweetheart . . . just one particular person,' he corrected explicitly over his shoulder.

Expelling a half vexed, half disconsolate breath, she returned to his front and gave the heavy bandage one last bracing tug to make it as secure as she could, pressed the two small attached hooks into the under-neath layer, then taped the adhesive plaster over the hooks in an effort to keep them in place.

Race looked down at her handiwork somewhat rue-fully. 'I am supposed to be able to breathe while I'm wearing this, you know,' he mocked.

'Pity,' she mouthed inaudibly, still smarting from his last remark.

'And, from your point of view, about to become very much more so!' he retaliated promptly, showing he had recognised her lip movements. 'Because now that there's nothing to interrupt you perhaps you would care to explain just how you and Grant came to be discus-sing my mother!' His eyes narrowed shrewdly. 'Was he worried that I might draw comparisons between the two of you? Is that why you were sent along to allay my suspicions?'

He was too close for comfort, except on one point. 'Not to allay them . . . to deny them completely!'

'With the flimsy excuse you had to offer?' A sarcas-tically peaking brow registered his disbelief.

'Sometimes the truth is less believable than a fabri-cated story, but that still doesn't make it any less the truth!'

'Then prove it!'

'Prove it?' she echoed, taken aback. 'How?'

'By resigning. By going back to where you came from and having nothing more to do with Grant.'

'*No!*' Her refusal was emphatic. 'Why should I give up such an enjoyable job, working for someone I like, just to assuage your suspicious mind?' Tilting her head to one side, she surveyed him consideringly, and not a little tauntingly. 'Or would it be your mercenary in-

stincts I'd be assuaging instead? That is why you'd like
to see me leave Grant, isn't it, Race? Because you're
frightened that imagined remuneration you mentioned
might include something you consider you're entitled
to? With Grant never having married, I bet you stand
to inherit the lot of this—you as good as own it even
now—but that state of affairs could change quite disastrously, from your standpoint, if he were to become
too fond of me, because men of his age have been
known to be extremely generous with their possessions
in such instances, haven't they?' She laughed disparag-
ingly. 'Why, you're no better than you accuse me of
being . . . out for whatever you can get!'

During her denunciation Race had been rocking back
and forth on his heels, a long-suffering expression on
his face. Now he came to an abrupt halt and fixed her
with an unwavering look.

'Have you quite finished?' he demanded caustically.

'Why? Have I hit a nerve?' Her countering question
was insolently voiced.

'Far from it. You're way off beam, as it so happens.'

'Oh, yeah?' she drawled in patent disbelief.

'*Oh, yeah!*' he took obvious delight in mimicking.
'You see, disappointing though you may find the information, I already happen to own Wanbanalong—
and everything on it—except for Grant's personal possessions.'

'But—but you can't,' Kylie stuttered helplessly, her
confidence nose-diving at a rate of knots. 'Grant said
the property was his!'

'And so it is . . . to live on, to come back to, to call
home,' he revealed with an exasperating smile. 'He just
doesn't *own* it any more, that's all. He sold out to me

over a year ago. Pity he didn't think to tell you, wasn't
it?'

He was too sure of himself for it not to be the truth,
and yet Kylie still couldn't quite bring herself to accept
it. 'Then why try and get rid of me by suggesting I
resign?' she questioned in bewilderment. 'Even if there
was something between us, it wouldn't affect you in any
way.'

'Except on principle! He's still an extremely wealthy
man—as I'm sure you're fully aware—and I've no wish
to see him fritter away what he does possess on you!'

'He only pays my wages!' she defended herself resentfully. 'Surely even you can't have any objections to
that.'

'You mean he's never given you anything extra?
Never bought you a gift of any kind?' he delved closely.

'Well—yes, he has,' she began hesitantly, too honest
to lie. 'But it was only something small. A trinket, no
more!' Her voice rose in dismay as a cynical look spread
over his face.

'To some women, diamonds are trinkets!'

Defeat was staring her in the face and Kylie sank
down despondently on to the bed. 'You just don't believe
a word I say, do you?' She shook her head incredulously.

'You're damned right I don't!' Race sounded quite
pleased with her final acceptance of the fact.

'In that case, I guess there's nothing more to be said.'
She rose slowly to her feet again and glanced at her
watch. 'It's late and I'd better start getting ready for
dinner.'

'That'll have to wait.' His arm came up to bar her
progress when she would have moved past him. 'I

haven't said you can leave yet.'

The dictatorial tone, more than the words, had her eyeing him mutinously as her indignation flared. 'Then I suggest you do so, because I'm about to leave!' she snapped. 'And don't think that just because you own this place you can order me around, Race, because Grant's still my employer . . . not you!'

'But you did agree to his loaning you to me for the duration of your visit, didn't you?' he reminded her silkily. 'Or would you prefer me to tell him you're only interested in working when there are ex gratia rewards in the offing?'

'Oh, yes, you'd like that, wouldn't you?' she seethed impotently. At the moment he appeared to hold the upper hand in every department. Tight-lipped, she swung away from him and resumed her seat on the edge of the bed, her whole attitude one of deliberately brazen provocation when she stared upwards to demand brashly, 'Well, what do you want done? Not that I would want you to think I was in any way dissatisfied with the situation, of course, but I don't exactly have time to burn myself, you know.'

'It isn't only time that will be burnt if you don't watch yourself,' he forecast threateningly as he headed for the adjoining bathroom with supple strides. In the act of closing the door behind himself, he smiled mockingly. 'I also wouldn't advise you to take it into your head to leave immediately my back is turned. Not if you know what's good for you, anyway. Why not just bide your time by making yourself useful and doing some tidying up, hmm?'

Kylie scowled furiously at the shut door and flounced to her feet to stand with her hands on slim hips, her eyes roving around the room. Tidying up what, for goodness' sake? The room was spotless except for his discarded shirt, and as there wasn't a clothes hamper to be seen—she presumed that was in the bathroom—she left it where it was. It did prompt her to remember that he hadn't taken a change of clothes in with him, however, and determined he wasn't going to dress in the bedroom, she walked across to the bathroom door and began hammering on it.

'Tell me what you're planning to wear and I'll pass them in to you,' she called.

'You hunt something out. I told you to make yourself useful,' his response came back above the sound of running water.

Pulling a disgruntled face, she turned her attention to the wardrobe, which surprised her with its lack of selection—and what there was, was in the main of a work nature—until she remembered that Race didn't normally reside on Wanbanalong. Eventually she extracted a pair of dark brown moleskins, a plaited leather belt, and a light green and fawn checked shirt. A pair of dress stock-boots she put beside the bed—she didn't mind him donning those in front of her—but she had to search through each compartment of the chest of drawers before she located some socks and underwear. The former she tossed on to the bed, and the latter she carried across to the bathroom, together with the rest of his clothes.

'These were the best I could find,' she said, opening the door a few centimetres and sliding them through the gap.

'They'll do,' he accepted them casually, and, the weight lifting from her fingers, Kylie withdrew her hand. Then, in an amused voice, 'What, no footwear?'

'I thought they'd be easier for you to put on out here.'

'Your consideration overwhelms me!'

Sarcastic devil! she denounced inwardly, and pulled the door closed with a vengeance.

It was a while before he finally appeared, but when he did Kylie's growing impatience with the lateness of the hour was suddenly forgotten as a broad grin replaced the annoyed frown on her face. He might have been dressed, but it was certainly only after a fashion, for he had missed at least one loop on his pants with his belt, his shirt was more out than in and with only the bottom two studs fastened, while his hair was a mass of tousled curls still dripping with water.

'Oh, my, don't we look smart!' Kylie just couldn't help teasing as she swung out of the chair by a writing desk where she had been flicking through a farming magazine while she waited. 'You really do need assistance, after all, don't you?'

'So it would appear!'

He couldn't have growled his disgust at having had his independence curtailed any more plainly if he'd tried and, as a result, Kylie's grin expanded into an uncontrollable smile of pure delight. She had found a chink in Race Brandon's seemingly impenetrable armour! He might have blackmailed her into helping him, but he actually disliked having to accept it more than she did giving it. She smiled again, pleasurably, but to herself this time. Perhaps she wasn't as weaponless against this man as she had been beginning to believe!

'You might at least have dried your hair a little more,' she reproved dulcetly as she collected a dry towel from the bathroom. 'It's dripping all over your shirt.'

'That's the least of my concerns,' he retorted.

A deeper nuance than usual in his voice had Kylie looking at him intently, and it was only then that it registered he was nursing his right arm in his left hand. On closer inspection she could also see that the muscles along his jaw were tense with strain, and she hurried the last few feet in alarm.

'For crying out loud, what did you do to yourself in there?' she demanded worriedly. 'Did you hit your arm or something?'

Race shook his head slowly, a ghost of a wry grin making an appearance. 'No, it's my collarbone. I think I've been without that sling for too long, and with this cast on it's giving me merry hell at the moment.'

'Then why didn't you say so immediately? Grant was right, you are a stubborn, independent fool!' she muttered crossly, tossing aside the towel and picking up the sling. Hurriedly she placed it halfway around his arm and then snatched it away again. 'Oh, for heaven's sake, sit down! I'll never be able to manage it properly while you're towering over me.'

'Sorry,' he apologised drily, but she guessed it must have cost him an effort, because he was very careful with his arm when he lowered himself on to the bed and the corners of his mouth pulled in sharply straight afterwards.

'There, is that better?' It hadn't taken long to knot the piece of supporting material at the back of his neck once he was seated, and now she angled her head to one side to look at him enquiringly, hopefully.

'A little . . . thanks,' he nodded ruefully. 'Give it time.'

'You should have gone in to wash as soon as you took it off.'

Some of the tenseness was starting to leave his features, but Kylie just wasn't prepared for the relaxed smile that suddenly swept across his well-cut mouth, and it set her heart pounding so heavily that she only just heard his acknowledging,

'So I realise . . . now! But I had other things on my mind at the time.'

She laughed unsteadily, still fighting to discipline her unruly feelings. 'Perhaps it will teach you the right order for your priorities in future.'

'Oh, I think the order was right. It was the timing that was wrong,' he countered enigmatically.

'If you say so,' she shrugged, not wanting to pursue the matter. For some unknown reason she was nervous of the answer he might give if she requested an explanation. Instead she picked up the towel and smiled faintly. 'I—I guess I'd better dry your hair, or else your shirt is going to be wet through.'

'I can do it,' he replied roughly.

'No, you'd better not take the chance.' She pulled it out of his reach when he would have taken it from her and began rubbing the wet strands vigorously.

Although he sat patiently throughout her ministrations, Kylie suspected he was anything but content with them, and the thought did a lot to restore her natural equanimity. It was such a change—not to mention satisfying—to have Race at a disadvantage that she fully intended to make the most of her opportunities while they lasted.

'Will you comb it, or shall I?' she queried artlessly when she had finally finished and replaced the towel in the bathroom.

Race didn't even bother to answer. He just gave her such a sparkling glance that she merely collected the implement from the dresser and handed it to him without another word.

'You're very adept with your left hand, aren't you?' she mused, watching him rake his hair efficiently into order. He certainly had been on those occasions when he had caught hold of her so swiftly. 'I suppose you've been getting a lot of practice.'

'Mmm, thirty-four years of it. I happen to be left-handed,' he divulged drily.

Strangely, that hadn't occurred to her. 'I guess that would account for it, then,' she half smiled, and returned the comb to its resting place. 'Now, what about your sleeves? Do you want them up or down?'

'Up.' He immediately set to rolling his right sleeve himself. 'I can't fasten this cuff over the cast when it's down.'

He had no choice but to let her attend to the other one, but in the end she wasn't able to decide which of them had been most chagrined by her assistance. Race, because he would have preferred to have done it by himself. Or herself, because it left her with a disconcerting desire to continue touching the brown warmth of his muscled flesh which she found more than a little unsettling.

In an attempt to hide her capricious feelings she bent and swooped upon his socks. 'These next?' she asked without quite looking at him.

'Thanks.' He relieved her of them and replaced them on the bed next to him.

After a few moments spent covertly watching him

struggling one-handed to fit a sock, however, her confusion was overcome by irritation at the pride which insisted he manage it on his own, and she pushed his foot off the bed—where he had been attempting to keep it propped—and back on to the floor.

'Oh, stop trying to be so damned self-sufficient!' she castigated testily as she dropped to her knees in front of him to begin sliding the woollen covering into place. 'What do you want to do, break your ribs again, bending over like that? Anyway, isn't this what I'm supposed to be here for . . . to act as nurse?'

'But not nurse*maid*!' he ground out explicitly.

Kylie sat back on her heels and looped a silky fall of lustrous chocolate brown hair behind her ear, the better to see him. 'It seems to me that whether you like it or not, Race Brandon, you don't really have any option in the matter,' she pointed out in a distinct purr.

Thick ebony lashes lowered fractionally. 'And that affords you no little satisfaction, does it, tiger eyes?'

'Oh, I wouldn't go so far as to say that,' she shrugged airily, and busied herself fitting his other sock. 'Although I must admit it does have certain possibilities.'

'But not for long, it would be as well for you to remember,' he counselled repressively. 'In a month's time you'll find the positions have very definitely been reversed.'

Her task accomplished, she looked up with wide provoking eyes. 'You'll be helping *me* to get dressed?' she quipped facetiously.

'I shouldn't think so. Grant might consider that an encroachment on his rights.'

'Then it's a pity you didn't think of that a while ago

before you kissed me!' she fired back immediately, springing to her feet, and bitterly resentful that he should have chosen to answer in such a manner. 'Your only concern then, I seem to recall, was the satisfaction of your own uncontrolled libido!'

'Hardly uncontrolled, sweetheart,' he retorted mockingly. 'My injuries preclude anything too undisciplined.'

'Well, three cheers for small mercies! Maybe every cloud does have a silver lining, after all,' she gibed.

Race pushed his feet into his elastic-sided stock-boots and leisurely gained his feet. 'Except that you're going to be deprived of yours shortly.'

'Meaning?' She eyed him warily.

'Only that you've made all you're going to out of Grant, and that the next time he goes touring I mean to make certain you're not around to go with him.'

'Oh, and just how do you propose to do that?' she scoffed, confident of Grant vetoing any such effort.

'With guile would be most appropriate, don't you think? since that's no doubt how you obtained the position for yourself in the first place.' He executed a taunting smile which sent prickles of nervous apprehension scraping down her spine. 'So how do you think you'll fare in a match of wits with someone who's wide awake to your little caper, huh, tiger eyes?'

'I—I'll manage,' she asserted throatily, but not altogether convincingly. Just the thought of being engaged in such a contest with him was enough to have her questioning her ability to defeat him. 'In the meantime, though,' her voice grew a little stronger now, her gaze not quite so uncertain, 'would you mind very much not calling me by that ridiculous name?' she requested sarcastically. 'My eyes are nothing at all like a tiger's.'

'No?' His brows lifted in expressive contradiction. 'I suggest you take a good look in the mirror, sweetheart, because that's exactly what they're like. Tawny gold, with dark enigmatic pupils, and flashing defiance the minute anyone stands in your way.'

'The same as any neighbourhood tabby?' she half laughed derisively.

He smiled lazily, goadingly. 'Except that on this occasion I was talking about your eyes, not your morals.'

Kylie's cheeks burnt with a fiery hue. 'Oh, I was right the first time, you *are* despicable!' she almost shouted in her bubbling anger. 'How dare you make such an outrageous insinuation! You know nothing about me or my morals, absolutely nothing, do you hear? And if you think I'm staying here to listen to any more of your offensive remarks, you can damned well think again!' Storming across the room, she flung open the door, then turned to face him again. 'And while you're fixing your belt, why don't you try hanging yourself with it, you—you contemptible reptile!'

The unrestrained laughter engendered by her wistful suggestion had Kylie slamming the door shut even more forcibly than she had opened it, and she stomped down the hall muttering all manner of imprecations under her breath. So much for attempting to convince him of her innocence! From now on he could believe whatever he liked and to hell with him!

CHAPTER THREE

AFTER having been detained for so long, it was only by hurrying frantically that Kylie managed to shower and dress in a becoming frock of rose pink dacron that tied at the shoulders with shoestring knots leaving an expanse of smoothly tanned skin bare, and join Grant and his nephew, as well as their guests, before the others had entered the dining room. There hadn't been a hope in the world of her making it in time for an aperitif.

Selena and Victor Walmsley, she discovered, were father and daughter, not husband and wife as she had supposed when Race mentioned them, and the family resemblance between the two was very strong.

Victor was a tall, heavy-set and grey-haired contemporary of Grant's; his daughter only a few inches shorter and built on statuesque lines. Although she was dressed in an obviously expensive gown of oatmeal silk, it was of a particular shade and style that Kylie privately considered did absolutely nothing for Selena's dark colouring or her somewhat voluptuous figure, but which considerations she gathered from the other girl's manner and conversation were the least of Selena's concerns.

Apparently there was only one interest in Selena's life—the land. How to tend it, how to make it produce better and faster, and how to obtain more of it. In this latter regard Kylie had a sneaking suspicion that Race was considered the prime solution to the problem with a union of the two families through marriage. Not because there was any love involved—one got the impression that such feelings were a sign of weakness to Selena's way of thinking—but because it made good business sense.

As she took her seat at the table Kylie couldn't help wondering just what Race himself thought of the idea. Would he be interested in such a calculated alliance? Somehow he didn't seem the type . . . and yet it wasn't unknown for holdings to be enlarged in such a fashion. Money went to money, and if he hadn't found anyone he loved enough to marry by now—or should that have read, could *trust* enough to marry? she grimaced sardonically to herself—then perhaps those were the only circumstances under which marriage *would* interest him.

It was an inexplicably disquieting thought, but one she was glad she wasn't given any time to dwell on further as her attention was claimed by the man facing her across the table.

'You're from the Gold Coast, Kylie, I believe Grant said,' smiled Victor sociably.

'That's right,' she nodded with a reciprocal curving of her lips. 'From Surfer's.'

'You'd notice a difference in the scenery out here, then,' he half laughed.

It was so reminiscent of what she herself had said only that afternoon that Kylie couldn't forbear a swift glance towards the watchful figure at the end of the table, just to her right, to see if Race recalled it as well as she did. From the glittering green look she received in return she presumed he did, and with an impudent uplift of the corners of her mobile mouth, she turned back the other way.

'Oh, yes, they're certainly as different as chalk and cheese, but it was quite surprising really that the further west we came the more I felt a kind of affinity for this awe-inspiring outback landscape,' she replied sincerely. The smothered grunt of scorn which came from her right she disregarded completely. 'In fact, I'm very much looking forward to seeing more of the country hereabouts while I've got the chance, as well as the inland regions of Queensland when Grant and I set off again.'

'Well, you'll probably never have a better opportunity to see everything in this area if you're going to be driving Race around for the next . . .' Grant paused and sent an enquiring look down the table. 'How long is it exactly before that strapping and cast come off, Race?'

'Another three weeks to a month,' came the wryly sighed response. 'Nevertheless . . .'

'Now I hope you're not about to say that there was no call for us to have returned again,' interposed Grant from the opposite end of the polished table as Abby began serving dishes filled with slices of chilled melon. 'I know the first two weeks were no doubt the worst, but even you'll have to admit that just having an extra pair of hands to do the driving is going to make it that much easier for you.'

'And there must be dozens of other little ways in which we can make ourselves indispensable,' added Kylie, oozing helpfulness.

'Such as?' Race's eyes narrowed suspiciously.

She had hold of his dish of melon before he was even aware what she was about. 'Why, by cutting up your food for you,' she beamed.

'Thanks very much, but I've managed for myself until now.' He made to take it back, but Kylie wasn't having any of that and moved it further away.

'But only with difficulty, I'm sure,' she warbled sweetly, setting about the fruit with a flourish. 'And it's not as if I haven't had any practice.' A highly goading glance was directed his way from the cover of long, curling lashes. 'My sister's two young children often experience problems handling their cutlery too.'

He didn't reply—at least, not vocally—but there was no doubt in her mind that he was saying a few choice words inside, and she applied herself to her task assiduously. First points to her, she adjudicated happily. Above her head Race caught his uncle's eye.

'Actually, I wasn't going to say that you shouldn't have come home,' he denied lazily, referring to Grant's previous remark. 'But that, if I were you, I would seriously think twice about retaining Kylie as your driver/companion when you do start travelling again.'

It was hard to say which of the other four at the table looked the most surprised, but it certainly had the effect of making Kylie snap upright again, the melon suddenly forgotten.

'What makes you say that?' frowned Grant.

'Yes, I'd be interested to hear your reasons as well,' she glared. She hadn't anticipated him putting his stated intention into motion so soon, nor so openly.

Selena and Victor merely looked curiously from one end of the table to the other.

'I'm only thinking of what's best for you, sweetheart,' Race explained with mock-regret. And to Grant, 'I just consider that it would be wiser if you had a male companion once you get off the beaten track ... for protection, if nothing else.'

'Protection from what, for heaven's sake?' quizzed Kylie mockingly. 'You don't think we're likely to be attacked by a lone kangaroo wanting to try its hand at a bit of boxing, do you?'

'No, I was thinking of another type of animal altogether,' he relayed in a taunting tone. But his next words weren't bantering, they were deadly serious. 'Namely, the two-legged kind who's capable of taking a life for any number of reasons, some not even comprehensible. There have been campers who've come to such an end in the outback. A case in point occurred only a couple of years back, if you recall?'

'Well, y-yes, of course I do,' she confirmed, once everyone's general recollections had been aired. 'But something like that happens so very rarely that you can't let the fear of it rule your actions. I mean, according to statistics, we're all more likely to become victims of road accidents, but that doesn't stop us from driving cars or walking across streets.'

'Besides, the case you're talking about happened quite close to a town, didn't it?' Grant enquired of his nephew. 'We're only planning on camping when there's no other choice available. At least, I am,' he half laughed.

With a sigh of relief that her employer didn't mean to meekly accept Race's proposal, Kylie resumed her dissection of the fruit in front of her.

'That would make a difference,' reflected Victor thoughtfully.

'Provided, of course, that Kylie is well versed in emergency procedures,' inserted his daughter, somewhat squashingly. 'There are other dangers in going bush, don't forget. What about vehicle breakdowns, being caught in a bushfire, or if, for instance, Grant was bitten by a snake? Would Kylie know how to treat him?'

In the face of this new attack on her capabilities, Kylie looked up quickly. 'I think so,' she claimed steadily. Handing back the dish of now finely cut melon, she received an exceedingly dry, 'Thank you,' for her pains, but her attention was concentrated on the girl opposite. 'Although I've never seen it done in practice, I know that you apply a tourniquet as soon as possible, then cut—the . . .' She faltered to a halt on seeing Grant give a warning shake of his head from the corner of her eye and Selena's mouth widen in a scornful smile.

'Good lord! You are behind the times, aren't you?' gibed Race mockingly. 'The old cut and suck routine went out at least ten years ago. Even the tourniquet and wash method is old hat now.'

Kylie chewed at her lip uncomfortably and looked to her employer for help. 'Then how . . .?' she murmured helplessly.

'By applying firm pressure over the bitten area with a broad bandage—and as much of the affected limb as possible—then immobilising it with a splint which you leave on until you reach medical care. But you don't cut, suck, or wash it, nor do you affix a tourniquet,' he advised ruefully.

'But if you don't use a tourniquet, what prevents the venom from reaching the bloodstream?' she puzzled.

'The pressure on the wound which delays its movement, and by keeping the limb as still as possible. You see, the latest research has shown that snake venom travels through the body by way of the lymph system, not the venous system, as was previously believed,.'

Kylie digested the information with a musing nod, then followed it with a triumphant smile which she directed towards the man on her right. 'Yes, well, now I *do* know how to treat snakebite, don't I? That's one emergency problem disposed of ... *if* it should ever occur!' She began slicing into her own fruit with evident satisfaction.

'Mmm, except that my concern wasn't brought about by the thought of any natural hazards,' Race unerringly reminded them of his original argument.

'And you're exaggerating the possibility of any other kind!' retorted Kylie swiftly. She knew his underhand reasons for doing so too! 'Good grief, you live in the outback! You, more than anyone, should know just how unlikely it is that anything untoward would happen.'

'It's because I live here that I can see the inherent risks involved,' he countered smoothly, vexingly. 'To some extent the outback is still a haven for those who would rather—how shall I put it?—keep a low profile for a time?—and although the majority of them are harmless enough, it only takes one who isn't for you to have trouble.'

'Even so, I still think you're making mountains out of molehills,' she grimaced. 'Grant obviously didn't have any such fears or he wouldn't have hired me.'

'Maybe Grant had other things on his mind at the time.'

The blatant innuendo had her glaring at him furiously, while his uncle laughed lightly, 'Mainly, a desire to have someone else do the driving. However, if the idea of our camping worries you that much, then we'll forgo it. 'There's no problem.'

Victor pursed his lips consideringly. 'I would have thought you'd have to camp if you mean to visit some of those areas you talked about.'

'While I'm still inclined to agree with Race that a male companion would be more suitable,' put in Selena. She smiled apologetically. 'No offence intended to you, Kylie, of course. I'm sure you would do your best. It's just that I do feel for a trip such as Grant plans that both of you need to be able to perform any task that's likely to require doing.'

'For example?' Kylie enquired in wry tones. She had no doubt that Selena had something specific in mind, although why the other girl should have been going to such lengths to prove a case for a male companion she had no idea. But one thing she did sense: Selena wasn't doing it out of concern for either Grant or herself.

'Well, changing tyres would be one.'

Kylie swallowed the piece of fruit she had been chewing and smiled broadly. 'I worked in a service station for three years, Selena, and I can assure you I've seen enough tyres changed to know how to do it.'

'Ah, yes, but I wasn't doubting that you know how to change one, what I was meaning was, *can* you change one on that four-wheel-drive of Grant's?' the older girl emphasised pointedly. 'We have one the same and, believe me, the tyres are so heavy it takes me all my time to lift one on to the axle when the vehicle's jacked up. Personally, I don't think you would have a hope at all of succeeding.'

'Maybe not, but I can,' interposed Grant protectively.

'Which is exactly the point I'm trying to make,'

Selena impressed on him earnestly. 'What if you were injured and couldn't do it? You'd be stranded! And all because you didn't have anyone capable with you.'

'Perhaps that is a point which needs to be considered,' pondered Victor heavily.

'Not until it's been proven, though,' Kylie demurred defensively. 'I would at least like a chance to try it first. I'm not exactly a puny weakling.'

Race nodded his thanks to Abby, who was collecting the now empty dishes, then allowed his gaze to slide appraisingly over Kylie. 'You're no Amazon either, sweetheart,' he drawled drily.

Was that a compliment, or a complaint? Coming from him, she really couldn't believe it would be the former, and she merely shrugged deprecatorily by way of a reply. As far as she could see there was nothing to be gained by pursuing the subject, and the sooner the conversation was steered into less contentious channels the better pleased she would be. If they were given enough opportunities, it was all too conceivable that either Race or Selena might very well come up with a valid reason for Grant considering a companion of his own sex might be more advantageous after all.

Abby's return with their next course of pineapple glazed ham, golden roast potatoes, buttered carrots and mint peas fortunately diverted everyone's attention for a while as Grant proceeded to carve the meat and the various dishes containing the accompaniments were passed to and fro across the table.

Kylie watched surreptitiously as Race went about filling his plate, but immediately he had finished he caught her completely unawares by picking up the plate and offering it to her.

'To save you the trouble of trying to catch me off guard,' he taunted, but not so loud that anyone else could hear.

Recovering quickly, she retaliated in kind. 'You just don't want to admit what a good job I did on the melon.'

'I don't know about that, but you've certainly done a good job on Grant.'

'Meaning?'

He uttered a low, rueful laugh. 'You've got him well and truly convinced you're the only companion he wants for this trip of his, haven't you, tiger eyes?'

'I do my best,' she quipped banteringly.

'Perhaps too good a best, I'm thinking,' he conceded, to her surprise.

With knife and fork stilled for a moment she cast him a hopeful glance. 'You're not by any chance admitting defeat, are you?'

'Uh-uh!' He moved his head from side to side slowly but decisively, the challenging look in his green eyes setting her heart pounding to a hectic rhythm. 'There's more ways of getting from point A to point B than by just travelling in a straight line.'

'Devious ways, is that what you're suggesting?'

His ensuing smile in no way helped Kylie to put her wayward emotions back on an even keel. 'What's good for one is surely good for the other,' he alleged ironically.

'Only nothing I've done *has* been devious,' she retorted, righteously indignant.

One dark eyebrow quirked implicitly. 'Not even the reason behind your offer to cut my food for me?'

'I meant, in my relationship with Grant,' she parried,

even as her cheeks flushed with colour.

'*Race!*' Selena's voice, filled with impatience, broke in on them suddenly. 'Do you think you could please stop whispering to Kylie long enough for someone else to have a word with you? I've tried twice now and been ignored both times.'

'I'm sorry,' he smiled pacifyingly at her. 'What was it you wanted?'

'About the tennis party next weekend,' she supplied sharply, her tone clearly indicating that she wasn't completely mollified. 'The arrangements were made to hold it at Elouera Springs before you had your accident.'

'And . . .?' he prompted.

'Well, I've had a couple of enquiries these last few days—I'm the secretary of our local Club,' she advised for Kylie's benefit in a smug-sounding aside.

'As well as being our best player,' inserted Victor with some pride.

Selena preened unashamedly beneath the praise. 'Apart from Race, of course,' she simpered. 'But where had I got to? Oh, yes, the enquiries. People have been asking me if we'll still be playing at Elouera Springs, or if the venue is to be altered.'

'I can't see why,' Race shrugged impassively. 'Although, to be quite truthful, it had slipped my mind. I'll have to get in touch with Adrian to make sure the court's prepared, and to let Mrs Hirst know, but otherwise there's nothing to stop it taking place as planned.'

'Oh, good!' Selena smiled her satisfaction, then just as swiftly pressed her lips together irritably and continued, 'But why you insist on keeping that vinegary old Mrs Hirst around, I really don't know. She must be eighty if she's a day, as deaf as a doorpost, and about as useful as a broken rubber band. All she ever does is make waspish remarks, and it never fails to amaze me that you're willing to suffer the inefficient and cantankerous old termagant when, if Grant moved over there with you, you could just as easily have Abby instead, who would do the work twice as well in a quarter of the time.'

'Now, Selena ...' her father immediately remonstrated with a cautioning frown, and Kylie, happening to choose that moment to return Race's plate, gave a sigh of relief to know that the flash of icy anger in those green eyes wasn't about to be directed at herself. Nonetheless, and much to her amazement, there was none of it evident in Race's voice when he spoke, only a wry type of forbearance.

'Old age is something that, unfortunately—or perhaps I should say, hopefully—comes to all of us, Selena,' he reminded her patiently. 'Mrs Hirst can't help being a little less efficent nowadays, nor is it her fault that her hearing is failing. As regards her—um—testiness at times ... well, I can only say that I very rarely encounter it, and as she's always been the closest thing to a mother I ever had, then I certainly don't intend to turn her out just because she's served her purpose and is getting old. As far as I'm concerned, she has a home at Elouera Springs for as long as she wants it, and irrespective of whether she's competent or not.'

Kylie inwardly cheered his sentiments, but Selena obviously wasn't impressed, nor silenced by his championship of the woman. 'Well, to my mind it's totally unbusinesslike to continue paying for services you're no longer receiving,' she declared. 'But if you're determined to keep her there, you should at least reduce her wages to a minimum and then employ someone else who can do the work proficiently. The homestead will soon deteriorate if its supervision remains in her hands.'

Race acknowledged her remarks with a sardonic inclination of his dark head. 'Thank you for the advice, Selena, but I think I'm quite capable of deciding for myself what staff I need, and how much I should pay them. Mrs Hirst certainly isn't that inept, and for the time being I can see no reason not to leave matters exactly as they are.'

Heaving a reluctantly resigned sigh on this occasion, Selena relinquished the topic and turned her attention to Kylie instead.

'I don't suppose you'd play tennis, would you?' she asked.

It was a negatively worded enquiry and Kylie's lips formed a wry smile. The statuesque brunette sounded as if, having scored a loss against Race, she was now looking for a victory wherever she could find one.

'Well, yes, I do, as a matter of fact,' she consequently took pleasure in disclosing. 'We do occasionally do other things on the Gold Coast beside surf and sunbake, you know.'

The light sarcasm was lost on Selena. 'But what type of tennis? The hit and giggle kind?' she proposed contemptuously.

'Mmm, I'm afraid our Wednesday nights did sometimes degenerate to that extent,' Kylie was willing to concede. What she didn't reveal, however, was that the grade games she played at the weekends were never anything but serious, hard-fought contests. That information she decided to keep to herself until she discovered just what Selena had in mind.

'You could, with an effort, play a whole game without breaking up, though, I presume?'

'Oh, yes,' Kylie nodded, keeping her amusement to herself. 'I have been known to go through a whole match without once finding anything to smile about.'

'Well, in that case, I guess we could fit you in a game or two next Sunday, seeing that you'll be there anyway,' Selena allowed ungraciously. 'Adrian needs a partner for the mixed doubles since Pam Shields is away on holiday, and I expect he'll be willing to take anyone as his partner rather than just forfeit the competition.'

Only the chance of a sweeter revenge in the not too distant future prevented Kylie from throwing the disparaging offer—if it could be called that—back in the other girl's face.

'Thank you,' she gritted as pleasantly as possible. 'And I can assure you I'll do my best not to let said Adrian down.'

'At least you're lucky he's a good loser. He won't shout and blame you, even if it is your fault.'

Not trusting herself to reply to that remark without showing any of her escalating irritation, Kylie sought another tack. 'Just who is this Adrian I keep hearing about?' she enquired of them generally. 'That's the second or third time I've heard his name mentioned.'

It was Race who answered. 'He's my trainee manager-cum-bookkeeper. You'll probably meet him at the sale tomorrow.'

'Oh, are we going to a sale?' Her eyes swung towards Grant for verification. 'Where?'

In response he smiled and gave an uninformed shrug. 'You'd better ask Race that, but I'd say in Broken Hill, most likely.' He looked to his nephew to query interestedly, 'Are you buying or selling?'

'At a guess, I reckon he's thinking of buying . . . the same as we are,' interposed Victor with a wry laugh. 'Henry Burbridge is having a dispersal sale, and you know what bloodlines he's always bought, don't you?'

'Wanganella,' nodded Grant sagely. Then, with a frown, 'How come Henry's selling out?'

'Well, he wasn't getting any younger, and now his daughters are all married and living elsewhere—and having no son to carry on after him—he figured there wasn't much point in holding on to the place any longer,' Victor explained. 'I know his eldest girl has been on at him for some time now to go and live with her and her husband, so I presume that's what he's intending to do.'

'Then if it's a dispersal sale it won't be held in Broken Hill after all, but on his property,' assumed Grant, and received an affirming nod from his friend.

'Oh, that's a pity,' Kylie exclaimed involuntarily, and couldn't help looking a little disappointed.

'What makes you say that?' quizzed Race curiously.

She hunched one shoulder selfconsciously. 'Only because I was looking forward to seeing the Silver City.'

'You know something about the Hill then, do you?' he drawled, referring to her use of the town's nickname.

'A little. But what you read about a place is never as satisfying as actually seeing it first-hand.'

'In which case, you'll be pleased to know I have an appointment in there late tomorrow afternoon, so you'll be able to see your Silver City after all,' he advised equably.

Kylie returned to her meal with a pleased smile, until she heard Aelena demanding in a denigrating tone,

'What's so fascinating about Broken Hill, anyway? It's only a mining town when all's said and done.'

'Well, apart from the fact that it happens to be the headquarters of both the Flying Doctor Service and the School of the Air in New South Wales, it also happens to be sited along the richest silver-lead-zinc deposit in the world. That much I do know,' Kylie replied. 'Besides, the fact that it's so isolated and it serves such a vast and intriguing region makes it a place of interest as far as I'm concerned.'

'They don't allow women down the mines, if that's what you're hoping for,' Selena tried squashing from another quarter.

'That's a relief!' Kylie had no hesitation in destroying her supposition with a significant grimace. 'Although I have the greatest admiration for those who work underground, I've never once experienced the slightest desire to see their work areas. I don't usually suffer from claustrophobia, but I have the feeling I could quite possibly, knowing all that rock and dirt was above me.' She glanced from one end of the table to the other. 'Just how far down are they? Do any of you know?'

Selena promptly shrugged indifferently; Grant and Victor lifting their shoulders not so much in disinterest as ignorance; and it was left to Race to supply, 'The last I heard was thirty-seven levels. Just over one and a half kilometres.'

'That settles it, then,' Kylie laughed shakily. Even the thought of being that far below the surface made her nervous. 'I definitely have no wish to venture down a mine. I much prefer to have the ground underneath me, not vice versa.'

'My thoughts entirely,' admitted Victor gruffly.

For some minutes the conversation lapsed as they all did justice to Abby's culinary efforts, then Selena just had to insert another of her hopefully disappointing comments.

This time it was, 'You do realise, of course, that there's nothing left of the "broken hill" which gave the town its name, don't you? There's just huge mounds of worthless tailings there now.'

As Kylie had already guessed as much, the information didn't really worry her one way or another, but before she could say so Race had begun to speak.

'I don't know that I'd exactly call them worthless, Selena,' he contradicted drily. 'What with the new processes of extraction, etcetera, these days, I hear there's still quite some money to be made from those dumps.'

'Yes, well, that may be so,' she conceded dispassionately. 'I just meant that Kylie shouldn't expect it to look anything like it did originally. When the old-timers were discovering silver lying on the ground in other areas close by, and used to decry it by derogatorily referring to it as a "hill of mullock", they had no idea how prophetic those words were going to be.'

'And no doubt many of them heartily wished they'd paid it more attention when it was finally realised just how rich an ore body they'd been ridiculing for so long,' he laughed.

'Who did eventually discover it?' put in Kylie swiftly, becoming absorbed in the subject.

'Ah, now that I *do* know,' said Grant in pleased accents. 'It was a man by the name of Charles Rasp, and the year was 1883. He was a boundary rider on Mount Gipps Station who used to do a bit of prospecting on the side. Actually, he thought he'd found tin until he received the assayer's report on the sample he sent away to be analysed.'

'Whereupon he promptly gave up boundary riding,' she surmised with a grin.

'Mmm, and as he retained his original interest in the syndicate of seven which was formed to develop the leases he'd pegged out, he understandably soon became an extremely wealthy man,' he continued with an answering smile. 'In fact, it was he who commissioned the Silver Tree to be made from some of the first silver taken from the mine, and which is now permanently on display in the Civic Centre.'

'Why, particularly, in the form of a tree, though?' she puzzled.

'Because he wanted it to be typical of the country where the ore was discovered. It's a beautifully detailed piece of work standing almost a metre high, and with figures of kangaroos and emus, wallabies and sheep, aboriginals, and a stockman on his horse all set out around the tree's base.'

'But that's what I'm getting at,' she couldn't help smiling. 'If there's one thing lacking in the landscape out here, it's trees. Apart from those planted around the homestead, there's hardly any.'

'Now!' interjected Race laconically from her right, and had her turning to look at him with a frown.

'You mean, there used to be trees out here? Then what happened to them all?'

His lips twitched wryly. 'They went up in smoke.'

'In a bushfire?' she put forward doubtfully. Very rarely did they destroy trees completely, and especially not on such a vast scale.

'In furnaces for the mine smelters,' he divulged

matter-of-factly. 'Unfortunately, the region was even more isolated in the early days than it is today, so the only fuel available to them was wood, with the result that, apart from the regeneration reserves which have been planted around the city to prevent soil erosion and those hellish dust storms which used to be synonymous with Broken Hill, the plains within a hundred-kilometre radius are just about treeless. Not that it was ever heavily wooded, of course—it just isn't that type of country—but by all accounts, it certainly did used to have more trees than it has now.'

'I see.' Kylie was silent as she chewed thoughtfully through another couple of mouthfuls. 'But wouldn't that make it hard on your stock? Having so few trees for shade, I mean.'

'Oh, of course not!' broke in Selena scornfully, and appearing to take the harmless remark as a personal affront to her farming techniques. 'There's plenty of places where sheep can find shelter. Beneath acacia bushes, under mulgas, in among the saltbush, down gullies, behind rocks, any number of places.' She gave a supercilious smile. 'Trees even, where there's permanent water.'

Kylie acknowledged the information contemplatively, and although there were many other questions she would have liked to ask, she decided against voicing any of them. With Selena doing her best to show her up as both incapable and ignorant, she would probably be doing herself a favour if she waited until she was alone with Grant before asking what she wanted to know.

Consequently, during the remainder of the meal, it was only when topics of a general nature were introduced that she joined in the conversation, but when they adjourned to the sitting room afterwards and, at Victor's instigation, Selena began playing the piano for them, Kylie would gladly have exchanged the perform-ance for a lively verbal attack.

At the keyboard Selena was definitely no virtuoso, and the piece she had chosen to play was so dreary that it required a superhuman effort just to stay awake. After her third surreptitious yawn Kylie glanced drowsily round the room to see if it was affecting the others the same way.

Grant, she noted, had his head laid against the back of his armchair and his eyes closed, but whether he had actually dozed off she couldn't have said. Not un-expectedly, since it had been his suggestion, Victor was proudly engrossed in watching his only offspring. While Race, who was perched on a stool beside the bar at the rear of the room, was just as speculatively assessing her own features, she discovered with a start.

When he eased to his feet and crossed the room quietly towards her, Kylie watched his approach with a wide-eyed wariness which totally dispelled her prior feeling of sleepiness. For one reason or another, thus far she had only found Race's company to be extremely unsettling, and she didn't envisage this occasion being any different.

'Aren't you a fan of classical music?' he drawled lazily, softly, out of the side of his mouth as he lowered himself on to the two-seater couch beside her.

'Yes, I am, as a matter of fact,' she whispered back primly, pinning her eyes to the silk-covered figure at the piano, and then mutely cursing the involuntary reflex that made her yawn yet again. Selena's interpretation of this particular piece was certainly doing nothing for her, though.. 'It—it's just been a long day, that's all. Grant and I were on the road very early this morning. We covered almost seven hundred kilometres to get here today.'

Race stretched his left arm indolently along the back of the couch. 'And all so you could offer your services that much sooner, eh?'

'Not that you seem to appreciate it,' she muttered tartly, nervously aware of his hand so close behind her.

'Oh, but I do,' he alleged whimsically, his fingers beginning to twine absently among the silky strands of her hair. 'How could I have possibly made it through dinner without your invaluable and so expert assistance?'

For the first time since he had sat down Kylie swung around to actually look at him, intent on delivering a pithy retort, but on encountering those rich emerald green eyes filled with provoking glints, all she could do was to stare at him helplessly and attempt to swallow the suffocating lump which had risen in her throat. What new form of attack was he planning now? she asked herself in agitated despair.

'Well . . .?' he probed in taunting tones.

'I expect Selena would have been a willing substitute.' Her voice was low and husky when she was finally able to get the words out.

'Uh-uh!' He denied her assumption with an idle shake of his head. 'It would never have occurred to her. Selena believes we should all battle on for ourselves regardless.'

And was that another reason why he had been so reluctant to accept any help from her? Kylie mused gloomily. Because he knew Selena wouldn't approve?

The thought should have been a satisfying one considering her prime objective in offering her assistance so assiduously had been to annoy. But it wasn't. Unaccountably, it left her with an empty feeling inside which disconcertingly precluded any sensation of pleasure.

'And you agree with her, naturally,' she murmured sardonically. Her attempts to free her hair unobtrusively from his fingers were proving disturbingly unsuccessful.

'Do I?'

'Well, don't you?'

'I thought I'd just said how grateful I was for your efforts during dinner.'

'Mmm . . . sarcastically!' she retorted with a grimace. 'Which hardly makes it particularly believable.'

The corners of his mouth curved upwards into a heart-stirring smile. 'While your motives for offering assistance were purely altruistic, I suppose?' he countered drily.

Even though she had the grace to blush, Kylie was determined to deny his attraction, at least this time, and she kept her gaze challengingly high. 'Maybe not entirely, but even if they had been, you would have suspected otherwise.'

'You're sure of that?'

'Oh, yes, I'm sure!' Her temper began rising at his deliberately goading questions. 'But, quite frankly, I don't give a . . .'

'S-ssh!' He caught her by surprise, both by grinning and by laying a cautionary finger across her lips, as her voice unconsciously became louder. 'Or Selena will think you're not interested in listening to her recital.'

Almost on cue the girl at the piano directed them a direful look, faltered, and fortunately had to return her attention to what she was doing. Not so Victor and Grant, however. Their faces remained turned towards the couch for a few seconds longer, Victor's wearing a somewhat offended expression, and Grant's a decidedly quizzical one.

Kylie sank farther down into her seat in embarrassment and glared resentfully at the man beside her. 'Go away!' she mouthed at him silently.

In reply his eyes gleamed with unabashed laughter and he motioned for her to move closer with a beckoning forefinger. Her vehement refusal was made in the form of a vigorous shake of her head, but Race obviously didn't intend to be thwarted that easily, and an inexorable hand on the nape of her neck succeeded in forcing her unceremoniously nearer.

'What on earth do you think you're doing?' she gasped, straining to regain some distance between them.

'I thought that would have been obvious,' he bent his head to murmur beside her ear. 'I'm trying to talk to you.'

'Well, I very much doubt you're likely to have anything to say that I want to hear,' she sniped.

'Is that final?'

Disregarding the slight inflexibility which had crept into his voice, she nodded swiftly. 'Yes!'

'Okay.' He shrugged as if it was a matter of complete indifference to him and released her. A few seconds later, without saying another word, he had levered himself upright and returned to the stool by the bar.

The suddenness of his withdrawal left Kylie floundering in an ocean of confusion. Conversely, now that he had gone she found herself wishing she hadn't been so hasty in refusing to hear him out. Not that she intended giving him the satisfaction of guessing as much, and with this in mind she resolutely forced her features into an uncaring expression and pretended a rapt concentration in the remainder of Selena's wearying performance.

CHAPTER FOUR

'I've just seen Race, he'll be along in a minute,' advised Grant when Kylie joined him in the dining room for breakfast the following morning. 'In the meantime, though,' his eyes held hers speculatively, 'just what was that all about between the pair of you during Selena's impromptu concert last night?'

'I'm not sure myself really,' she shrugged. 'Why don't you ask Race?' He had been the instigator, after all.

'I already have.' His admission was heavily sighed.

'And?' warily now.

'I might just as well have saved myself the bother. Where you're concerned, I can't get a word out of him. And therefore,' he paused significantly, his tone incisive, 'I think it advisable you have your promised talk with him no later than today, Kylie, before this situation gets out of hand altogether. Otherwise I'll be doing it for you whether you want me to or not, I'm sorry to say.'

Kylie shakily returned the cup she had been about to fill with coffee to the sideboard. 'But I have spoken to him,' she protested. 'I saw him before dinner yesterday and tried explaining to him then.'

'*Tried* explaining?' he emphasised questioningly, iron grey brows drawing into a frown.

'He—he didn't believe me,' she stammered uncomfortably.

'Because you were still wanting to teach him a lesson

68

and, consequently, didn't make your effort very convinc-ing?'

'No!' she denied earnestly. 'I said I would try, and I honestly did. He just chooses not to believe me, that's all.'

'And you were going to leave it at that? Why didn't you tell me this last night?'

He sounded less tolerant by the minute and Kylie moved restively beneath his lowering gaze. 'I—well, there didn't seem to be anything that could be done about it.'

'We'll see about that!' Grant deposited his half filled plate on the sideboard and began striding purposefully for the door.

'You're not going to say anything to him?' she queried worriedly, starting after him.

Stopping, he nodded sharply. 'My word, I'll be saying something to him! This has gone on quite long enough and I mean to put a stop to it right now. It may have had faintly amusing overtones yesterday, but the longer it continues the less humorous it becomes. And that goes for your part in it too.' He shook his head in self-annoyance. 'I knew I shouldn't have let you over-ride my better judgment in allowing you to explain in-stead of doing it myself.'

Left chewing at her lip anxiously, Kylie watched his departure with dejected eyes. She shuddered to think what Race's reaction was likely to be at being taken to task by his uncle—if that was, indeed, what Grant planned—but even more worrying was what Grant's attitude might be when he returned. With Race no doubt urging her dismissal, coupled with her employer's recent rebuke regarding her part on the misunderstanding, wasn't there a likelihood that as the cause of the dissension between him and his nephew she could find herself out of a job after all?

Absently she returned the food from Grant's plate to a warming tray, her thoughts otherwise engaged. Had he found Race yet? What was he saying? What was Race saying in return? She trembled involuntarily. Was he reminding his uncle how pleasant and placid everything had been before she arrived on the scene, or was he so damned furious he couldn't think straight? Whichever it was it didn't augur well for her, she brooded cheerlessly.

She was still standing in the same spot when Grant returned, nervously, with Race keeping step beside him, and her wide and apprehensive eyes darted from one to the other. To her surprise they both appeared relatively relaxed compared to what she had been expecting, and she immediately started biting at her lip again. If Race wasn't uptight that surely meant things had gone his way and, that being the case, rather than meekly wait for the axe to fall she preferred to know the outcome as soon as possible.

So, with a brittle half smile catching at her mouth, she eyed them bravely. 'D-do I get a chance to resign, or—or . . .'

'Resign?' Grant broke in incredulously, and not a little testily. 'For heaven's sake, what's come over you? Why would you want to resign now?'

Race calmly began ladling steak and eggs on to a plate. 'I rather think it's not so much a matter of Kylie wanting to resign, as of being under the impression she's about to be fired,' he put in sardonically.

'You can't be serious!' his uncle exclaimed, astonished. And to Kylie with a frown, 'Is that true? Were you expecting to be fired?'

Relief that she apparently wasn't about to be rendered Kylie speechless and all she could do was nod, shakily.

'But why? I never even considered dismissing you, let alone mentioned it.'

'No, but . . .'

'But she thought I might have persuaded you to,' Race inserted impassively, and causing Kylie to glance at him in surprise. She hadn't expected him to be so open about his previous intentions.

'Ah, now I'm beginning to understand,' Grant nodded him comprehension ruefully. 'But fortunately, that's all in the past now . . . *isn't it?*' A glowering gaze encompassed both of them. 'And that's where it's going to stay too, so why don't you . . . If you were two men I'd suggest you shake on it and start again,' he half laughed wryly.

'So what do you propose in our case, that we kiss and make up?' quizzed his nephew in the driest of tones.

Kylie stepped in smartly, extending one arm. 'I think a handshake will be quite suitable,' she asserted in a slightly throaty voice. No matter what had been said between the two men, Race's attitude was no less disturbing than it had ever been, and whether he was being sarcastic or not she didn't intend giving him any leeway.

Almost as if he could read her mind Race smiled lazily, his emerald eyes taunting as her proffered hand was engulfed by strong brown fingers. Together with the warm hard contact, his smile had Kylie's senses fluttering agitatedly and she removed her hand as quickly as possible from his grasp.

'Right!' Grant rubbed his hands together pleasurably. 'Maybe now that's over and done with we can get on with breakfast.'

Once they had repaired to the table Kylie waited to see how Race fared with his food, and although he was managing after a fashion it was obviously a long and laborious struggle, and just as obviously he wasn't about to seek assistance. For a time she was able to ignore it, but for some unknown reason she couldn't do so indefinitely and, eventually, she just had to say something.

'You know, you really are the most obstinate person I've ever met,' she sighed. 'Don't you think it would make it an awful lot easier if you just asked for help with that?'

'I didn't know if it was allowed ... under the new rules,' he parried mockingly, but seemingly relieved to be able to hand his plate across all the same. 'And I wouldn't want to be accused of jumping to the wrong conclusions again.'

'No, of course you wouldn't,' she agreed on a wry note, picking up his knife and fork. 'I can see how badly it's shattered your self-assurance.'

His well shaped mouth tilted satirically. 'I notice yours doesn't appear greatly impaired either, tiger eyes,' he drawled.

'Now, now!' Grant's call for order came from the other end of the table. 'Don't tell me you two are at loggerheads again!'

'By no means,' Race denied blandly. 'We were merely discussing—er—characteristics.'

'Hmm!' His uncle's eyes narrowed astutely as he took in the pair of them. 'There's some of those *I* wouldn't mind discussing too, only we don't have the time this morning. Not if we're going to make it to the sale on time, that is.'

Kylie replaced Race's plate in front of him, and discovered him to be eyeing his relative with some amusement.

'Now I wonder what caused that sudden change of mind,' he smiled speculatively. 'I thought you intended giving it a miss in order to spend a restful day at home.'

'Yes, well, maybe I've decided it would be more restful if I accompanied you,' retorted Grant meaningfully.

Race started to laugh. 'Don't worry, I wasn't planning on wreaking vengeance on your little protégée immediately you were out of sight. She won't need your personal protection.'

Certainly Kylie hoped not. Up until that moment it hadn't even occurred to her that she might!

'I still think I'll go anyway,' said Grant, albeit in a trifle abashed manner. 'If Henry's leaving the district altogether, it could be the last chance I'll have to see him before he goes.'

'Apart from the farewell party which is bound to be held for him.' Race's reminder was drily made.

The older man clearly felt he had been on the defensive long enough, because he now leant forward to challenge, 'Are you trying to say you would rather I didn't go with you?'

'You know better than that,' Race grinned, totally unperturbed. 'In any case, if it should run later than planned—which is quite on the cards—I might ask you to stay on, if there's something worthwhile bidding for, when we have to leave for town. I could ask Adrian, but he hasn't quite got the experience in that line yet, and I must admit I'd prefer an older hand at it.'

'That could be arranged, I guess,' Grant acceded, and patently pleased at the thought of being able to help. 'But this appointment you mentioned, what's that for? Something to do with the properties?'

'No, these.' Race gestured towards his injuries. 'Derek wants to check on their progress.'

'Have they been giving you some trouble?'

'Not so much of late, although there were some twinges yesterday.'

'Oh, yes, that's right . . . in the office,' frowned Grant at the memory.

Kylie's gaze intercepted an extremely wry green one being aimed her way and she promptly pretended concentration on the last of her meal. She strongly suspected it wasn't that occasion, but another later in the day, which Race had been referring to.

'It certainly doesn't hurt to make sure,' Grant went on thoughtfully. 'If there is something amiss, it would be better to have them broken again and re-set now, rather than later.'

At that, Kylie's eyes flicked upwards faster than she had previously dropped them. 'There's no likelihood of that being necessary, though, is there?' she queried anxiously of Race. She dreaded to think that might be the result of her attempts to annoy the day before.

As if from a distance she heard Grant's sobering, 'The possibility's always there if they're still giving him pain,' but it was the answer from the man on her right she was waiting for and she continued to look to him worriedly.

'I doubt it,' he smiled reassuringly, giving her cause to sigh with relief. 'Although, whatever the outcome, I think you'd better stop looking so harassed. Nurses are supposed to cheer their patients, you know, not alarm them.'

Now that her fears had been somewhat allayed Kylie could afford to retaliate in kind. 'Mmm, but nurse*maids* can't help feeling concerned when their charges will insist on overestimating their capabilities,' she bantered provokingly.

From Grant's puzzled countenance it was clear he was having difficulty in associating their remarks, but from the sparkling gleam in Race's eyes it was obvious he was having no such trouble.

'You'll get yours, sweetheart,' he promised tauntingly beneath his breath as he reached for his coffee.

'And, let's hope, so will you,' she whispered back daringly.

They weren't the first to arrive at the Burbridge property by any means. There were vehicles of all kinds already parked beside the homestead and groups of people—mostly men, Kylie noted—strolling haphazardly all over the place.

Race and Grant immediately began making for the holding paddocks and yards down by the woolshed, stopping frequently to greet and introduce Kylie to friends, and waving acknowledgment to others. Some of the sheep had already been separated from their fellows and were penned in ones and twos, and half dozen lots beneath a lacy-leaved pepper tree, and it was here they came across Adrian Cresswell, Race's trainee manager.

In his late twenties, with dark blond hair and humorous grey eyes, he was an extremely personable young man who obviously enjoyed an extremely good rapport

with his employer and was well liked in the community.
In fact, Kylie was to decide very shortly, it would be
nearly impossible not to like someone as amiable and
goodnatured as Adrian.

'Oh, by the way,' she grinned at him as they trailed
their respective employers on their round of the pens,
'Selena's picked me as your doubles partner for tennis
on Sunday. I hope you don't mind.'

'Not in the slightest,' he returned with an appreciative gaze. 'I'd say I was to be congratulated.'

'But you don't even know if I can play,' she laughed.

'Well, can you?'

'I can.'

His ensuing sidelong glance was wryly amused. 'You
said that as if you really meant it.'

'I did,' she verified simply.

'You mean, you can *really* play tennis?'

She nodded expressively.

Adrian's delighted and uninhibited burst of laughter
caused not only Race and Grant to turn back to look at
them quizzically, but a good many others as well, most
of their gazes becoming indulgent on seeing two such
happily glowing faces.

'Oh, that's priceless, that is,' he grinned when his
mirth had subsided somewhat. 'I bet Selena doesn't
know.'

'No, she seemed determined to believe it was an
effort for me to get the ball back over the net,' Kylie
confided drily.

'I gathered as much, otherwise she wouldn't have
paired us together. You see, it's Selena and Brian Antill
we'll be playing against in the Club Championship
round.'

'I see,' she acknowledged musingly. 'And as your regular partner is away she's planning on a walkover for herself, is that the idea?'

'Something like, I should imagine,' he nodded. 'Selena enjoys winning.'

'Who doesn't?' Kylie quipped laconically. 'But just how good are they as a team?'

'They're good, make no mistake about that,' he counselled seriously. 'Of course, Selena usually plays with Race, and that's an even stronger combination— they've been Club Champions for the last three or four years—but I would have to say Brian follows him as a close second among the male players. His serve may not be as powerful or as accurate, but he's got a pretty consistent all-round game.'

'And Selena?'

Adrian pushed his wide-brimmed hat back and scratched at his head meditatively. 'If you're looking for weaknesses I should think lack of court coverage would be hers. She's not a particularly fast mover, although being so tall she does have a good reach. Normally her absence of speed doesn't worry her too greatly, though. She just slams her opponents off the court,' he concluded with a wry half laugh.

'And in doubles, of course, she doesn't need quite so much mobility,' Kylie murmured. Then, with a sigh, 'I wish they had a court at Wanbanalong. I haven't played at all for some weeks now and I think I'm going to need some practice if we're to give them a run for their money on Sunday.'

'Well, that's no problem,' Adrian denied promptly. 'Why not come over to Elouera Springs a couple of afternoons and we can practise there together? It will at least give us some idea of each other's games.'

'Oh, that's a great idea,' she approved enthusiastic-
ally, but as her glance happened on the two men some
distance in front of them a little of her eagerness began
to wane. 'The only thing is, I'm supposed to be driving
Race around wherever he wants to go. I don't know
whether I'd be able to get away.'

His brows arched humorously. 'Why don't you just
try asking?'

'Mmm, I suppose I could.' Grant, though, not Race!
'Which particular days would you suggest?'

'All the same to me,' he shrugged affably. 'How
about Thursday and Friday?'

'I'll see what I can do. Meanwhile . . .,' she began to
laugh, 'perhaps you'd better tell me how to get there. I
wouldn't have a clue where Elouera Springs is.'

Before he could comply, however, they caught up
with Race, who had stopped and was waiting for them,
and his voice reached out ironically.

'As much as I can understand your desire to socialise,
Adrian, I would like to remind you that we're here on
business. And as for you, sweetheart,' he swung his
mocking gaze in Kylie's direction, 'I'd appreciate it if
you could try to be just a little less distracting, then we
might all be able to concentrate on what we came for.'

Adrian immediately sent her an apologetic smile for
having to desert her, and with a rueful, 'Sorry,' for his
employer, headed for the pen Grant was presently in-
specting.

Kylie merely scowled.

'That'll do nicely,' endorsed Race aggravatingly. 'Try
and keep it up, hmm?'

'Go to hell!' she muttered resentfully. New rules or

not, it didn't appear to have lessened his sarcasm any!

About to move off, he fixed her with a goading glance. 'With you around, where else could a man possibly expect to be?'

An expressive grimace at his departing back and Kylie followed after him moodily. So he was disgruntled with her presence, was he? Well, she wasn't exactly exhilarated with his either! And whose fault was it, anyway? None other than his! If he hadn't been so anxious to believe the worst then none of this would have happened.

'Morning, Kylie! Where's Race?'

The deep bass voice brought her out of her reverie with a start, and on looking up she found herself confronted by Victor and Selena.

'Oh . . . good morning,' she smiled faintly, including them both. 'Er—he was over there a minute ago,' motioning towards the pen the others had last been viewing.

'I can't see him,' he frowned, trying to peer over the heads of the increasing crowd. 'But never mind, if we wander over that way I expect we'll run across him. Are you coming too?'

'I shouldn't think so,' broke in his daughter with a condescending smile. 'That's probably why Kylie's not with Race now. There wouldn't be much point in her depriving a legitimate buyer of a place on the rails when she obviously knows nothing at all about sheep. Anyway, I imagine she's finding it very boring.'

They were just the type of remarks needed to spur Kylie's previously flagging interest in the proceedings and she shook her head decisively. 'Quite the contrary, in fact. I'm finding it most informative, and although I admit I know very little about the wool industry at present, it's only by paying attention at functions such as this that one improves one's knowledge, isn't it?'

'Very true,' affirmed Victor with a smile. 'So, shall we go?'

As the sale was almost due to begin there was a considerable crush of figures surrounding the first yard now, and it took a while for the three of them to ease their way through the talkative crowd to where they could see Race, Grant and Adrian in conference.

Selena determinedly headed for Race's side, but somehow amidst the greetings and general rearranging, it was Kylie who wound up pressed between Race and his uncle, instead of on Grant's other side as she had planned. When she made a move to alter the positioning she felt her arm ensnared within an unyielding grip.

'You just stay where you are, tiger eyes,' Race bent to command softly, but no less compellingly for all the muted tone. 'I prefer you where I can watch what you're up to.' Quite without warning, he slanted her an engaging smile. 'And while you're about it, stop looking so incredibly sulky, huh?'

She widened her eyes facetiously. 'I thought that's how you wanted me to look.'

'Uh-uh! You were wearing a decidedly irritable expression before. At the moment I'd say it's nearer to being provocative, and unless you want it kissed off those charmingly pouting lips of yours I'd suggest you remove it very smartly.'

It was astonishment which had her eyes rounding now, as well as a touch of dismay that she could find the prospect vaguely exciting rather than displeasing. With a hasty swallow she spared a swift look at the number of people around them and squeaked almost inaudibly, 'You wouldn't dare!'

One well defined eyebrow peaked meaningfully. 'Is that a challenge?'

'No!' she gulped in panic. 'See, it's gone already.' And to prove her point she flashed him a brilliant, if a trifle impudent, smile.

'Mmm, I can see I shall have to remember that for future reference.'

'Remember what?' she chanced in puzzlement.

'That the threat of being kissed makes you extremely tractable,' he drawled indolently.

Kylie drew in a deeply indignant breath, but as the auctioneer began his preparatory speech at that moment—drawing Race's attention—there was little she could do except exhale it again slowly, while promising herself retaliation at a later date.

Soon the sale itself got under way and the bidding started, but it was such a practised routine that Kylie could neither distinguish the amounts the auctioneer was calling out, nor could she discern just which of the men crowded around the yard were making the bids.

To a novice it was all very bewildering, and when the sale of the first ram was concluded and the agent's assistant made a note in the papers on his clipboard, then acknowledged, 'Sold to Race Brandon of Elouera Springs for . . .' it was impossible for her to hear what else he had to say because she was just too stunned to listen.

With a disbelieving shake of her head she looked up at the man beside her. 'Did you buy that?' she demanded peremptorily.

At the near accusing note in her voice he grinned.

'Why, wasn't I allowed?'

'But—but I didn't even realise you were bidding! You didn't move at all.'

'Oh, yes, I did. You just weren't watching.'

'I was so!'

'Then you weren't doing it closely enough, were you?' mockingly.

'Apparently not,' she grimaced wryly. 'But when you're not quite sure just what you're looking for, it's very difficult. You might at least give me some clues.'

Since she hadn't really expected him to acquiesce, it came as quite a surprise when he obligingly explained the procedure, and she listened to all he had to say with pleased interest.

After that it certainly made it less confusing for her, and by the time an hour or so had passed she was becoming almost as quick as the auctioneer to detect which of the people present were potential buyers and which were merely spectators. It did take her a little longer to become accustomed to the separate methods of signalling bids, however, for they were almost as diverse as the crowd. Some used an almost imperceptible nod, while another might scratch his ear, or just slightly raise one finger, but as far as she could see there was never a definite gesture to draw undue attention.

The next purchase Race made was of a pen of ewes, but on the succeeding pen he dropped out of the bidding three-quarters of the way through and they were eventually sold to someone else.

'Well, that's it for me for the moment,' he advised with a relaxed flexing of broad shoulders. 'How about you, Victor?'

'No, I think I might take a look at the next couple of lots as well,' the older man replied. 'Where are you heading, to get a drink? We'll see you over there shortly,' he declared on having received a nod in confir-, mation.

'Why didn't you continue with your bidding on those last ewes?' Kylie asked curiously of Race as all four of them began moving towards the homestead.

'Because the price was being forced abnormally high,' he shrugged. 'Some people tend to think that because it's a dispersal sale you must be getting a bargain, no matter what the price. To my mind, that's a good way of putting yourself out of business.'

'And the ram, was he reasonably priced?'

'About what I expected.'

'Do you ever breed your own?'

'No, I'm a woolgrower, not a stud breeder.' He started to laugh as a result of all her questions and glanced humorously across to Grant. 'Haven't you told her anything about what you've been doing for the last forty years?'

'If I have, it appears it was all irrelevant information,' came the smiling reply.

'It's okay for those to talk who were born out here, isn't it, Kylie?' Adrian defended gallantly. 'But there's a tremendous amount to learn for those of us who weren't.'

'Oh, don't you have a country background either?' She looked to him in amazement. 'I automatically as-sumed you must have had.'

'No, I come from Melbourne originally. I only started jackarooing when I was nineteen.'

'And still couldn't ride properly when he arrived here

five years later,' growled Grant in amiable disgust.

'Don't remind me,' Adrian grinned.

'But I expect you've no doubt improved since then,' Kylie surmised encouragingly. As she had never even been on a horse the least she could do was support someone who had tried, since she suspected riding was rather more difficult than it appeared.

'Actually, I wish you hadn't said that,' Adrian's lips twisted ruefully as he looked towards his employer. 'There's some at the moment who would probably consider that's debatable.'

Race didn't say a word, just returned the look expressionlessly, and with a furrowing of her forehead, Kylie quizzed, 'Oh? How do you mean?'

Adrian cleared his throat deprecatingly. 'It was—er—due to my incompetence that Race is strapped up the way he is,' he disclosed with a sheepish look. 'That day out on the ridge, I let my mount cut right in front of his, which sort of left his with nowhere to go but down.'

'You didn't tell me that,' cut in Grant, eyeing his nephew accusingly.

'Would it have altered the outcome?'

'Maybe not, but it is nice to know all the facts.'

'What facts are they you're talking about?' enquired Selena, catching up to them in time to hear Grant's comment. As her father wasn't with her, Kylie supposed the other girl had abandoned him in favour of keeping Race in sight.

'None in particular, we were just generalising,' Race replied blandly. 'Have you come to join us in a drink?'

'I thought I might,' she affirmed, falling into step beside him. 'It was getting a little warm down by those yards.' She sent him an interested glance. 'Have you finished your bidding for the day?'

'Just about, apart from a couple I might ask Grant to handle for me.'

'Why Grant?' She stared at him in surprise. 'Where will you be?'

'I was thinking of getting Kylie to drive me in to town straight after lunch, instead of waiting until later,' he informed her. 'That all right with you, Grant?' He sent his relative a faintly amused sidelong glance.

Knowing full well the reason for that mocking enquiry Grant looked wry, but he agreed willingly enough. 'Certainly. I'll get Adrian to drop me off on his way home.'

'An early trip to town suit you too, tiger eyes?'

It was the first time Race had used that nickname so publicly and Kylie nodded selfconsciously as she felt the warmth of colour surge beneath the smooth skin of her honey-gold cheeks. Why he had altered his plans she didn't attempt to hazard a guess, but the thought of spending the whole afternoon in his company immediately began to assume perturbing proportions. The more so as she came to realise she was actually looking forward to it, when all her instincts for self-preservation were warning her that any entanglement with Race Brandon could only be to her disadvantage. Just because he wasn't openly hostile towards her any more— no doubt for Grant's sake—it would be as well for her to remember that didn't necessarily mean he had changed his mind about her.

CHAPTER FIVE

As good as his word, Race had them on the road and heading for Broken Hill immediately they had eaten, and once Kylie had carefully negotiated the unmade road leading from the Burbridge property to the highway, she was able to increase speed without fear of receiving any extremely speaking glances from her passenger—as had happened on a few occasions that morning—whenever she had inadvertently driven over a pothole.

'How far is it from here approximately?' she queried for interest's sake.

'Nearly fifty kilometres.'

'So that would make your place about seventy to eighty kilometres out, would it?'

'By my place, do you mean Elouera Springs, or Wanbanalong?' he counter-questioned lazily.

'I meant Wanbanalong, actually,' she answered steadily, refusing to let him put her off balance so early in the piece.

'Then you'd be about right in your estimate,' he allowed casually.

Mention of his home did remind her of something which had intrigued her since her arrival, and now she voiced it curiously. 'Why didn't you return to your own home after your accident, Race? Do you prefer it at Wanbanalong?'

He hunched one shoulder offhandedly. 'No, it was

just more convenient at the time, that's all. I could safely leave Adrian to manage Elouera Springs for a while, but there's no one on the staff capable of doing the same for Wanbanalong. So, . . .' He shrugged again, significantly.

'Are you dropping hints that you'd prefer it if I was there?' he quizzed drily.

'No, of course not,' she demurred swiftly. In truth, nothing had been further from her mind. 'I was only wondering. Or was that remark prompted by a guilty conscience perhaps?'

'Over what?'

'Oh, nothing. Forget it,' she pleaded anxiously, cursing her impetuous tongue. In an effort to distract him she pointed to the side of the road. 'What are those pretty red flowers called? They seem to be everywhere.'

Race ran a hand roughly through his dark hair and expelled a heavy breath. 'They're wild hops,' he advised flatly.

Relief flooded over Kylie that he hadn't chosen to break the tenuous thread of tolerance which existed between them at the moment. 'And—and the tiny white ones?' she continued. It seemed a safe subject.

'Onion-flowers.'

Along with the blue, white, and yellow daisies scattered about—as well as runners of the eye-catching red and black desert pea—they made a very attractive picture as they strove for life in the richly red soil, but it wasn't a topic she could pursue indefinitely and she cast about urgently for another.

Before one came to mind a sudden flurry of movement at the side of the road caught her attention. 'Oh, look, kangaroos!' she exclaimed. But hardly had she finished saying it than a rueful grin began to chase its way across her softly moulded lips. 'I guess they're no novelty to you, are they?'

'Not exactly,' he averred in an indolent tone. 'Nor would I have thought they'd still be for you. You must have seen plenty of them on your drive out here with Grant.'

'Mmm, we did . . . and emus.' She lifted her slender shoulders in a deprecating gesture. 'But I'm still not blasé enough as yet not to comment whenever I see any. Probably because I'm never expecting them.'

'More used to suntanned bodies jumping out of the way of your vehicle, are you?'

'You could say that,' she smiled. There had certainly always been enough of them around.

The kilometres between them and the sunlit hills of the Barrier Ranges which beckoned in the distance were swiftly being eaten up now, and as they drew closer and closer Kylie's sense of anticipation grew.

'What time's your appointment?' she asked.

'Four.'

'And where were you—er—planning on going beforehand?'

'I thought that was your department,' Race returned in a slow drawl. 'You're the one who wanted to see the place.'

'You mean, it was on *my* account you decided to come in earlier?' she gasped, stunned. She had never even considered that his change of mind might have been for her sake.

'It would seem that way.' From his wry tone he sounded almost as bemused by his indulgence as she was.

'Then thank you,' she smiled at him quickly, sincerely. Abruptly, some of her enthusiasm began to fade. 'And how—how are you going to fill in your afternoon?'

His clear green eyes ranged over her pensive profile slowly, sardonically. 'I had intended accompanying you, tiger eyes. Or are you dropping hints again?'

Unbidden, her spirits immediately began to rise again. 'Oh, no, I'd much prefer to have you with me,' she asserted positively, then flushed in embarrassment. 'I mean—well, it's always nicer to have someone with you when you're sightseeing, isn't it? And—and especially if they're a local.'

'I guess so,' he granted, a hint of amusement in his voice which didn't help to make her feel any better. 'But don't let it fluster you, sweetheart. I do realise it's not my specific company you prefer.'

Since that was strangely exactly what she did seem to prefer, Kylie supposed she should have been thankful that he wasn't aware of it. Yet, at the same time, she didn't want him thinking her quite that ungrateful. But how to say so, without letting him know the true state of her feelings, could prove somewhat difficult.

'I wasn't flustered,' she began stiffly, well in control, but keeping her eyes determinedly to the front. 'And I'm sure I shall enjoy your company, provided . . .'

'This should be good,' he inserted with a half laugh.

'Provided you stop being so damned provoking!' she concluded on a rushed and less controlled note.

A goading grin pushed the corners of his mouth upwards. 'You prefer it calm and restrained, do you, tiger eyes?'

'Yes!' Her concurrence was unequivocal. When he

was being provoking he was also too damned fascinating for her to rule her errant senses. 'And please stop calling me by that exasperating name. That's provoking too!'

'But so appropriate.'

'Only to your way of thinking.'

'Mmm, but something you're going to have to put up with all the same, because *that* I don't intend changing.'

'You will the other, though?' Half a victory was better than none.

'We'll see,' he drawled noncommittally.

Kylie suspected that was the best she was going to get under the circumstances, but at least it was a definite improvement on his attitude of the day before, she consoled herself. Heaven only knew what Grant had said to him that morning, but she thanked him wholeheartedly for his effort on her behalf, for when only partially amenable, his nephew was quite something!

In due course the road began to wind its way between the low eroded hills of the ranges, and after Race had indicated the old stone-constructed Mount Gipps Hotel—sited on part of the original station where the discoverer of the wealth the property's 'broken hill' paddock had to offer had been employed—she knew they were fast approaching their destination.

The next point of interest they saw was the radio control station for the Royal Flying Doctor Service, an unpretentious building set on the side of the highway within its own neatly fenced surrounds, and with not a neighbour in sight. Except for the small sign out the front Kylie might have driven past without even realising its significance, but as it was she started to slow and turned to Race enquiringly.

'Do they allow visitors in?' she asked hopefully.

'They do, but I'm afraid you're too early,' he smiled commiseratingly. 'They only have one visiting session a day and that's at four o'clock.'

'Oh!' She wrinkled her nose disappointedly, and pushed her foot back down on to the accelerator. 'That's a pity since that's also the time for your appointment. I guess I shall just have to make do with seeing the School of the Air.'

It was plain Race was trying not to laugh, but in the end he couldn't help it. 'Sorry, but you're too late for that one,' he grinned. 'Their public session starts at nine-fifteen in the morning.'

'You mean I'm going to miss both of them?' she wailed.

'Well, at the bases you are, at least,' he shrugged.

'I don't follow you.' She shook her head bewilderedly. 'What do you mean, "at the bases, at least"?'

'Only that, if you're interested in hearing either of them, I'd have thought you'd be better off listening on the transceiver at home.'

Momentarily, there was complete silence inside the vehicle, then Kylie began to laugh at her lack of thought. 'Of course, you'd have one, wouldn't you? Goodness only knows why I didn't think of that for myself, but I just didn't.' She slanted him a eager gaze. 'Would you mind if I listened in on your set one day?'

'I think that could be arranged,' he smiled so tolerantly that her heart started to thump suffocatingly against her ribs. 'You could even join in the talk session if you've a mind to.'

'Oh, no, I wouldn't want to do that. In any case, I'd

probably be struck dumb immediately it was my turn to speak,' she confided ruefully.

'It often happens that way with newcomers to the network, but you get used to it. After a while it becomes no different from using a telephone.'

'I think I'll just take your word for that, all the same,' she chuckled.

At last the hills gave way to the plains again and Kylie could see the city spread out before them, its centre neatly bisected by the workings of the various mines, for it had literally grown up around the line of lode. It was a large, sprawling city—understandably, perhaps, considering there were no natural barriers to its expansion—ringed by green reserves of eucalypts and other native species, its streets wide, like most country towns, and tree-lined.

Nevertheless, by the time they had completed a comprehensive drive around the town it struck Kylie that there was something missing among those wide streets, although it wasn't until they had parked beside the modernistic Civic Centre with its distinctive sculptured steel monument outside, and were actually walking across the road, that it finally came to her just what had been niggling at her subconscious.

'You know, I don't think I've seen one drain in all the streets we've passed!' she exclaimed. The storm drains were very noticeable where she came from. 'Don't they have them?'

'It was decided it wasn't worth the expense,' Race half smiled.

'How do you mean?'

'Well, we only get an average of twenty-three centimetres of rain a year—if we're lucky—but we have a three-*metre* evaporation rate. So, as you might imagine, what rain does fall isn't around long enough to warrant a drainage system.'

'Now I understand,' she acknowledged, laughing wryly, then almost immediately followed it by the serious probing, 'Such a low rainfall must create enormous problems in keeping a city of this size supplied with water, though, mustn't it?'

'Not now, fortunately, since they've dammed the Darling River,' he explained. 'They pipe it in now from the Menindee Lakes system some hundred-odd kilometres south-east of here. In the old days it was a different story, however,' he continued sombrely. 'Then, water was so precious it was bought by the gallon for exorbitant prices. Even later, when Stephens Creek reservoir was created, there still wasn't an adequate supply, and every summer as the waters sank lower and lower another epidemic of typhoid would break out and the accompanying deaths would start all over again.'

'Poor devils! It's not much of a recommendation for the "good old days", is it?' Kylie grimaced.

'Mmm, I doubt anyone in this town would ever want to see them again.'

'Although they did like to remind themselves of its reason for coming into being, I gather,' she smiled, moving to a lighter topic, and indicating the street name on a nearby signpost.

'No, they didn't mind doing that,' he concurred with a reciprocating grin. 'All the early streets were called after the wealth they'd won from the ground. Argent is the main street, of course, and this as you saw is Chloride. There's also Sulphide and Oxide, Crystal, Cobalt, Beryl, Mercury, Graphite, Wolfram, Mica, and so on. The list is almost endless.'

'At least it's different,' she conceded lightly as they entered the building. 'But didn't they find gold round here too?'

'Further north,' he enlightened her. Crossing the foyer, they began mounting the stairs which led to the upper gallery. 'At Depot Glen on Mount Poole Station, to be exact, and although that only proved to be a single patch, it wasn't long afterwards before they'd discovered it in larger quantities at Mount Browne, Warratta, and Tibooburra.'

Kylie moved her head incredulously. 'The whole area must have been a prospector's dream.'

'As long as you were prepared to accept the privations that went with such an arid, sunbaked locality in those days!'

The pungent reminder did tend to tarnish the romantic picture such discoveries conjured up somewhat, Kylie admitted ruefully, but on reaching the top of the stairs all such thoughts were put out of her mind as she caught sight of the Silver Tree in its glass showcase and she moved forward to examine it eagerly.

Just as Grant had proclaimed, she found it was a meticulously fashioned work of art, and not only in the main figures but also in the tiny details of each leaf of the tree, the feathers of the emus, and even minute animal footprints within the painstakingly defined blades of grass. All in all, she decided, it was a beautifully made and extremely impressive memorial for any city to have to honour its beginnings.

On their way downstairs again her thoughts remained with the centrepiece for a while and, as a result, involuntarily returned to the past once more.

'But if, as I seem to recall Selena implied at dinner yesterday, Broken Hill wasn't by any means the first place they discovered silver hereabouts, just where was it originally found?' she queried thoughtfully.

Instead of immediately answering, Race angled her an exceedingly wry look. 'You're certainly intending to get your money's worth out of me this afternoon, aren't you?' he drawled.

'Well, I did warn you I preferred to have a local with me when I went sightseeing.' Her return glance was anything but penitent. 'Or are you just trying to cover up the fact that you don't know the answer to my question?' she ventured teasingly, eyes gleaming.

'After that, it would be no more than your just deserts if I refused to tell you altogether,' he threatened mockingly.

'But you will,' she pressed persuasively.

With their glances locking inescapably for a moment they came to a halt. Race was the first to start moving again, with a dismissive shake of his head.

'Mm, I think maybe I'd better,' he owned ironically.

Following a pace or so behind, Kylie was desperately attempting to direct her thoughts outwards. Away from the devastating realisation that had he cared to kiss her during that brief taut pause, she wouldn't have objected in the least. In fact, she suspected she would even have welcomed it!

Even so, perhaps the aspect which occasioned the most mortification was the idea that his swift extrication might have been brought about by his awareness of her wayward feelings. Now, in an effort to disprove any such thoughts he might have been harbouring, she forced a half smile of supposed casualness on to her lips and caught up to him midway across the foyer.

'Well, where was it found, then?' she questioned brightly, though not quite as steadily as she would have liked.

'At Thackaringa. The Pioneer mine.'

His answer, she noted, was short and perfectly controlled, even if it wasn't particularly encouraging, but she pressed on regardless.

'And the others?'

He shrugged, holding open the glass door so she could precede him into the street. 'I guess Umberumberka would . . .'

'Say that again!' The close to laughing demand was made almost without volition.

Signs of humour appeared at the edges of his mouth, and his manner relaxed slightly—to Kylie's relief. 'Umber-umber-ka,' he considerately split it into syllables for her.

'Thank you,' she expressed her appreciation softly, shyly. 'And then?'

'Oh, Purnamoota, Apollyon Valley, Silverton,' he listed patiently. 'After the first rush there was a whole spate of them, and quite often their finds came in forms of ore the world hadn't known existed until then. Not only was it slugs of pure native silver they were happening upon, but also silver chlorides, bromides, iodides, glance, and some of it yielding up to twenty thousand ounces to the ton.'

'Yet they still hadn't realised even greater riches were waiting to be found right here,' she mused in utter disbelief. It was impossible to comprehend just how they could have missed it!

'No, they continued to decry the great black iron-

stone outcrop as a "hill of mullock",' he smiled.
'Although it's ironic really that Silverton, which was
probably the greatest depreciator of them all in its
heyday, is now more or less a ghost town dependent
upon tourists from Broken Hill for its limited survival,
while its gaol is a showcase for relics collected by the
Broken Hill Historical Society.'

'A ghost town, you said? Filled with curios?' she queried, her sideways glance from beneath long lashes slyly
assessing.

'Mmm, that's what I said.' Race's eyes roamed leisurely over her expectant face, and then he grinned.
'You'd like to see it, I gather?'

'Could we? Is it far?' she probed breathlessly. Not
from excitement at the prospect, but as a result of that
fascinating shaping of his mouth which was causing her
insides to perform somersaults.

'Twenty-two kilometres or so, that's all.'

'Then we can go?'

Reaching the car, Race pulled open the driver's door
and Kylie slid on to the seat, her gaze raised hopefully
to his. 'I guess so,' he allowed forbearingly, and closed
the door behind her.

They left town by a different route from the one they
had used to enter it, and as they breasted a slight hill on
the way out Kylie couldn't help remarking, 'It's strange,
but while you're in town you tend to think you're in
just another suburban shopping centre, and then bang!
something like that suddenly confronts you.' She
nodded towards the vastness of the untouched country
which stretched as far as the eye could see in any direction around the city. 'Then you begin to realise just how
isolated you actually are.'.

'Maybe that's why the government decided on Broken Hill as the depository for the country's gold reserves during the Second World War,' he proposed drily.

'Did they really?' She spared him a quick look of interest. 'Down the mines, I suppose?'

'Uh-uh!' he vetoed lazily, amused. 'Underneath the floor of the gaol, as a matter of fact.'

A peal of low infectious laughter bubbled from Kylie's slender throat. 'Yes, well, I guess a gaol would be the last place you'd expect to find gold bullion,' she granted.

The remainder of the afternoon flew past much too swiftly for her liking, because although Silverton today bore no resemblance to the restless mining encampment of old which had abounded with tents and hastily constructed shacks, the few buildings which had been built of stone for permanence were an engrossing reminder of the once feverish community, and the wealth of material displayed in the restored buildings more than sufficient to have kept her occupied for a week let alone one afternoon.

Eventually, though, it was Kylie herself who brought all thoughts of further exploration to a finish when, after a desultory check with her watch, she exclaimed in anxious tones, 'Good grief, do you realise it's twenty to four? You'll never make your appointment in time.'

Race calmly lifted his wrist in order to refer to his own timepiece. 'You mean twenty past three, don't you?' he contradicted in apparent amusement.

'No, I make it twenty to four,' she repeated earnestly, and at something of a loss to understand what he found humorous in the situation. 'Look!' Holding out her wrist so he could see for himself.

To her puzzlement he seemed no more worried by that irrefutable evidence than he had before, and when he coolly proceeded to take hold of her wrist in order to alter the time on her watch to coincide with his she could only stand and stare at him, nonplussed.

'You'll probably find it easier if you keep the same hours as the rest of us,' he drawled banteringly, releasing her. 'We work on Central Time here, not Eastern Standard.'

'Oh, hell!' she half laughed ruefully, selfconsciously. 'Grant did tell me too, but I forgot clean about it.' She uttered a fully fledged laugh this time. 'No wonder I've been thinking you have late mealtimes out here!'

'Then that could have been your problem,' he conceded mockingly. 'Nonetheless, as much as I regret having to call a halt to your obvious enjoyment, I think we'd better be making tracks for town, anyway, tiger eyes.'

'Yes, of course,' she accepted his decision equably. 'I shall have to make certain I come out here again with my camera before I leave with Grant, though. I'd hate not to have a record of the place.'

Briefly, Race appeared not to have heard her as he stared absently towards the horizon, then, running a hand slowly around the back of his neck, he smiled perfunctorily.

'Yes, well—if you're ready . . .' He indicated that they should head back to the car.

With a nod Kylie started walking, her thoughts a little confused as to the reason behind his abruptly preoccupied behaviour. Fortunately, however, it seemed to disappear as quickly as it had arrived, because by the time they had reached their vehicle he was back to being his alert, captivating self again.

Their journey back to town was swiftly accomplished, but when Kylie made as if to park the car within the hospital grounds Race held up a staying hand.

'No, don't bother, just let me out. It won't be much fun for you waiting around here, so you might as well go down the street and have a look around. I don't doubt you'd like to.'

'But how will I know when you're finished?'

'Oh, give me forty-five minutes or thereabouts,' he suggested. 'I shouldn't be much longer than that.'

'You're sure?' she questioned doubtfully, coming to a halt outside the entrance.

'I'm sure,' he confirmed as he pushed open the door and stepped out. Shutting it again, he leant his left hand on the roof and bent to look into the interior. 'I'll meet you somewhere around here when you get back, okay?'

'Fine.' When he began striding lithely away, she called after him diffidently, 'I—I hope it goes all right.'

He turned, saluted her with a finger raised to the brim of his bush hat and accompanying the action with such an enchanting smile on his lips that she couldn't drag her eyes away, and continued on into the hospital.

Kylie expelled a wry sigh of disbelief at having adolescently allowed physical good looks to have such an effect on her and set the car in motion. Perhaps it was a good idea after all if she spent the next half hour or so keeping her mind occupied with less worrying subjects, she decided ruefully. Grant's nephew could be all too charming when he chose, but she hardly thought it was wise to have him filling her thoughts all the time.

Even so, to dispel him completely from her thoughts

was easier said than done, she discovered to her chagrin, for as she strolled along Argent Street looking
interestedly at the shops she was conscious the whole
while of waiting for the time to pass. In the end, after
her fifth check with her watch in as many minutes, she
judged that she might as well return to the hospital. She
really wasn't absorbing what she was seeing and, who
could tell, she shrugged to convince herself, maybe
Race would be finished by then in any case.

When she had driven back to the hospital and parked
outside, Race was nowhere to be seen, however, and she
prepared to wait patiently for him. But when a quarter
to five came and went, together with another half hour
besides, and still no sign of him, she began to grow
restive. What could have been keeping him? Had there
been some complication, after all?

Her mental processes continued along the same nag-
ging line. Could that have possibly been why Race had
been so introspective during those last minutes at
Silverton? Because the time for his appointment had
been drawing near and he had known that everything
wasn't as it should be? Of course, it could just have
been that he had had to wait before seeing the doctor,
but even so, surely it wouldn't take this long!

The next ten minutes seemed more like an hour to
Kylie, and by the end of it she was positive there was
something wrong. But now, as her anxieties grew, so
did her fears that Grant's prediction might have been
accurate in that re-setting was required—a thought
which didn't help when she was already being tor-
mented by the knowledge that at times her behaviour
on the previous day certainly hadn't had a beneficial
effect upon his injuries.

Finally the passive waiting became unendurable and, scrambling out of the car, she set off for the hospital entrance, intent on making some enquiries. Once inside she made directly for the reception desk where she was advised that no, Mr Brandon hadn't had to wait before seeing Dr Taplin, and that he was still in consultation with him—a not exactly calming piece of information since that eventuality had been causing Kylie's greatest concern. The query as to whether she would like a call put through to the doctor's surgery to inform Mr Brandon of her arrival she refused with a nervous half smile.

'Oh, no, there's—er—no need,' she stammered awkwardly. No matter what the outcome she doubted Race would appreciate having his visit interrupted in such a manner, and especially by her of all people. 'I—I'll just take a seat, thanks, and—er—wait.'

The woman on the other side of the desk smiled her acknowledgment and resumed what she had been doing, while Kylie wandered over to one of the chairs lined against the far wall to begin flicking unseeingly through a dog-eared magazine. There obviously wasn't much point in asking the woman if she knew whether Race had required further treatment. She was only one of the administration staff, and to question any of the nurses who periodically made their way along the corridor would probably prove just as futile, since there was no guarantee any of them were even working in that particular section.

With a dismal sigh Kylie crossed her legs and looked at her watch, then uncrossing them again returned the magazine to the table in front of her and picked up another. Each time a door opened somewhere along the hall she peered hopefully towards it, but when it failed to herald Race's return she would comb her fingers through her hair distractedly and go back to crossing and uncrossing her legs again, and inevitably checking the time.

On a couple of occasions she caught the receptionist looking at her curiously, which did at least have the effect of forcing her to restrain her unconsciously fidgeting movements, although not usually for long because as soon as the woman's attention was turned elsewhere they invariably began again. It was shortly after the last of these glances that two male figures appeared at the end of the corridor, and seeing that Race's commanding form was one of them, Kylie leapt to her feet in thankfulness and stood watching as the two men shook hands before going their separate ways. Race heading towards her at a loose-limbed, ground-covering pace.

'Are you okay?' he questioned roughly, frowningly, immediately on reaching her side.

'Me?' Her brows flew upwards in astonishment. 'I was about to ask that of you!' Frantically her eyes searched for any sigh of a new dressing, or something different about him.

Race laid an arm casually about her shoulders and began ushering her outside. 'Later,' he dismissed her remark negligently. 'First of all I'd like to know why Derek received a call to say that there was an extremely agitated and worried-looking young lady at reception who'd been asking for me.'

So the woman had rung through after all! Kylie wished she hadn't. She had known he wouldn't like it.

'I'm sorry you were interrupted,' she shrugged uncomfortably. 'Although I did say I would wait.'

'You didn't interrupt me, and that's not what I'm talking about,' she was informed in taut tones. 'I want to know why you were apparently in such a nervous state. You didn't by any chance prang the car, did you?'

The fact that his query was made with a thread of lazy indulgence in the tone rather than annoyance did nothing to dampen her resentment at the suggestion. 'No, I did *not* prang the car!' she flared, pulling away from him. 'And—and of course I was worried! Why wouldn't I be?' She blinked rapidly to clear away the wateriness which was suddenly obstructing her vision, and which she put down to their emergence into the strong afternoon sunlight. 'You were supposed to meet me an hour ago!'

'But you knew where I was!' He stared at her incredulously.

'Maybe I did, but that didn't tell me why you were so long, did it? I thought—I kept remembering . . .' She came to a halt, white teeth chewing at a soft underlip, but just had to ask, huskily, 'Are they all still okay?'

Substantiated by a nod, Race dragged his fingers through his hair in almost as much perturbation as Kylie had done with hers not long since. 'Oh, hell, I'm sorry, sweetheart! It just didn't occur to me that you might think something had gone amiss, or that you would even be back on time, quite frankly. I thought it more than likely you'd become absorbed in your sightseeing again and be late returning.'

'Well, I wasn't! I was early, as a matter of fact,' she returned huffily. 'I arrived back here at half past four!'

'Oh? How come?'

Recalling her reasons, Kylie promptly berated herself for giving him the opportunity to put her on the defensive and, on reaching the car, she slipped around to the other side so she could put more distance between them as she eyed him across the roof.

'Because I thought you might be early, and *I* didn't want to keep *you* waiting!' she evaded in a gibing voice.

'You needn't have either, if you'd just let me know you were here,' he pointed out wryly as soon as they had taken their seats inside.

'I didn't like to.'

'Why ever not?'

She hunched away from the question discomfitedly. 'I thought you'd probably take exception.'

'Up until now I thought that's been your main objective,' he drawled.

'And maybe it should have been this time too!' she retorted tearfully, hurt by his facetious attitude. 'I can see how the idea of my being concerned amuses you.'

Race half turned in his seat, his left hand reaching across to cup her warm cheek, his thumb smoothing away the dampness clinging to her lower lashes. 'Not amuses, tiger eyes, so much as amazes,' he corrected in a deep voice. 'Solicitude from you I just wasn't expecting.'

'I don't see why,' she countered rapidly—before he perhaps decided on a deeper analysis. 'You're a human being too, aren't you?'

Abruptly, his green eyes crinkled with wry laughter. 'I wasn't sure, after some of your remarks yesterday. I had thought I might have been demoted to some lesser species.'

Kylie snatched her head away from his touch and fumbled for the ignition key. 'Now you're just being provoking again,' she accused, seeking protection from his undeniable attraction behind a shield of vexation. 'I should have known it was too much to expect it to last.'

'Well, at least you can be thankful for one thing,' he imparted drily, leaning his head against the back of the seat and sending her a disturbingly mocking glance. 'It was nowhere near as provoking as I felt like being, believe me.'

Although a variety of retaliatory gibes immediately sprang into her mind, Kylie eventually voiced none of them. Prudence dictated that she would be well advised not to tempt fate by replying in a goading fashion, so she contented herself with an unimpressed grimace instead. Calm and restrained was the way Race had claimed she liked it, and that was the way she would be well advised to keep it!

CHAPTER SIX

KYLIE watched helplessly as the rocketing ball kicked up chalk before disappearing past her over the base line and, loosening her grip on her tennis racquet, she rested her hands on slim hips.

'You know, I always figure that shouldn't be allowed,' she half laughed ruefully at the man jogging towards the net from the other side of the court.

'What, an ace?' queried Adrian with a responding grin.

'An ace to take out the match,' she clarified with an expressive grimace, moving to join him. 'It doesn't give you even a chance to fight your way back into the game.'

'Mmm, that's what I was relying on,' he revealed openly, ironically. 'I'm afraid you play just a little too well for me to take any chances. As it is, I only just scraped home the winner.'

'I don't know about that,' Kylie disclaimed with a laugh. 'You beat me two sets to one.'

'But only, I suspect, because you're out of practice,' it was his turn to grimace. 'Even so, it was hardly by what you would call a convincing margin.'

'Convincing enough to make me the loser,' she reminded him as they began heading for the homestead.

On the wide latticed verandah which surrounded Race's graceful colonial-style home Mrs Hirst, the housekeeper, was laying out a tray of cooling drinks and appetising savouries.

'I thought you might like some refreshments before you start for home,' she said to Kylie as she and Adrian mounted the front steps.

'That's very kind of you, Mrs Hirst, thank you,' Kylie replied in a slightly louder tone than normal. The little old lady was certainly hard of hearing, but she definitely wasn't as deaf as Selena had implied, nor as waspish, in Kylie's estimation. At least, she hadn't been so far.

Pleasant though she found it sitting and talking to Adrian, after half an hour or so Kylie was very much aware of the light beginning to fade, and it wasn't long before she was regretfully offering her excuses and preparing to leave.

'If I don't go soon it will be dark before I reach Wanbanalong and I could end up getting lost,' she remarked humorously.

Adrian's blond brows drew together in a frown. 'Perhaps you'd prefer it if I drove over with you, then?'

'Oh, no, I was only joking,' she reassured him. 'Grant gave me pretty straightforward details of the route, and as I didn't have much trouble finding my way here, I don't suppose it will be any more difficult going back again.'

However, after an hour on the dirt road and night having fallen completely, Kylie started to wonder if those words hadn't been more prophetic than she intended. The landmarks Grant had given her seemed altogether different now that she was travelling in the opposite direction, and with her vision confined to the relatively narrow path illuminated by her headlights, she was eventually, reluctantly, forced into conceding that somewhere along the way she had missed a vital turning with the result that she had, indeed, managed to become lost!

She couldn't remember having passed through so many gates on her way over to Elouera Springs, nor of having driven across three stock grids in succession as she had just done, and with a sigh she swung the Patrol four-wheel-drive around in a wide arc and began driving back over the ground she had just covered. At one of those gates she must have turned into the wrong paddock.

But which one? That was the problem. If she didn't choose carefully she could find herself stranded out there for the night, since she didn't have an unlimited supply of fuel at her disposal. There hadn't seemed any need to top up the tank when she had left that afternoon because there had been plenty in it already for the round trip. How could she have known she would be doing a tour of every paddock Elouera Springs possessed? Or was she on Wanbanalong? Kylie smiled irrepressibly to herself in the darkness. For all she knew, she might just as easily be on neither one of them, but on somebody else's property altogether!

At each gate she came to now she searched for signs of another track. The only trouble was that she had become so disorientated that when she did finally discover one, she wasn't quite sure in which direction she ought to go. To her right, or to her left? Some distance in front of her she could just discern what looked to be an outcropping of weathered sandstone and, hoping fervently it was part of the same formation she had seen on her right earlier that day, she started moving again but keeping it on her left this time.

After a while she was called upon to stop the vehicle in order to open yet another gate, but as she fumbled with the chain fastening her spirits rose considerably. She definitely remembered this one all right! It had given her as much trouble this afternoon when she'd come through. Clambering back into the vehicle, she drove through the opening, returned on foot to close the gate, then set off again with more confidence than she had for some time. Now that she was certain she was on the right track she didn't have to take it quite so slowly any more.

By the time the homestead lights finally came into view Kylie was feeling distinctly pleased with herself for having found her own way back and, after parking the Patrol in its allotted bay in the garage, she headed for the house with a light step.

'And just where the hell have you been until this hour?' Race's formidable shape suddenly loomed up out of the darkness as she was about to step on to the unlit verandah, making her falter in surprise.

'Wh-why, over at Elouera Springs. Didn't Grant tell you?' Even though she had spent most of her time chauffeuring Race over the property during the last two days, it had still been Grant's permission she had asked for time off that afternoon.

Race didn't say whether his uncle had told him or not. Instead, he disparaged with a biting edge to his voice, 'But it was too much to expect you to have the decency to let anyone know you wouldn't be back in time for dinner, I gather?'

Kylie hunched one shoulder in a deprecatory gesture. 'I'm sorry if you were held up on my account, but I didn't intend to be so late.'

'The time just slipped past unnoticed while Adrian was whispering sweet nothings in your ear, did it?'

'No, unfortunately he didn't get the chance,' she retaliated just as sarcastically. 'We were too busy playing tennis.'

'In the dark?' Not even the dimness on the verandah could completely camouflage the disbelieving lift of his brows. 'Or has he had lights installed on the court since I've been away?'

'I wouldn't know! It was still light enough to see without any when I left,' she retorted.

'Come off it, sweetheart!' he censured scornfully. 'I *know* how long it takes to get from Elouera Springs to here, remember?'

'But not by the route I took, obviously!'

'Oh?' Sooty-framed eyes narrowed suspiciously. 'So just where else did the pair of you go this evening?'

'The pair of us? Oh, you mean Adrian!' Kylie shrugged with a deliberately taunting vagueness. 'Well, I really couldn't say where he's been. Come to that,' she pondered musingly, 'I couldn't say for certain just where I've been either.'

Within seconds she felt steely fingers wrap themselves about her upper arm and she was propelled unceremoniously towards the light streaming from the open doorway.

'Have you been drinking?' Race demanded in a rasping tone as his green gaze scrutinised her upturned features intently.

'Yes! Three large glasses, in fact!' she goaded, her resentment at his treatment growing inexorably. 'Of lemon squash!' Her amber eyes clashed defiantly with his. 'But even if it hadn't been, I'm not answerable to you for my actions, Race Brandon, and you've got no right giving me a third degree! I've said I was sorry for being late, but any explanations I reserve for Grant. Where is he, anyway? In the sitting room?'

'Probably! Although not here.'

Her lips pulled into a vexed line. 'Meaning?'

'Grant went visiting this evening,' he enlightened her mockingly. 'He's not expected back until later.'

'Oh!' The information caught Kylie off guard. 'That was a sudden decision, wasn't it?'

'Not really. It was decided before dinner and he waited as long as he could for you. He thought his *companion*,' acidly, 'might have liked to accompany him! But as you couldn't be bothered to return on time, he didn't have any choice but leave without you.'

'I wasn't late because I couldn't be bothered to return on time!' she denied heatedly, and unsuccessfully attempting to break the grip which was keeping them in such close contact. 'It was due to circumstances beyond my control! Well . . . almost,' she added with sardonic honesty.

At that last enigmatic amendment Race's fingers tightened inflexibly about her arm and he gave her a none too gentle shake. 'Okay, tiger eyes, how about you cut the riddles and start giving with some answers, huh?' he recommended in abrasive tones. 'And for starters, I suggest you begin by telling me exactly where you've been tonight!'

'How should I know?' she rounded on him sulkily, realising he meant to find out no matter what objections she might raise. 'I got lost!'

'What do you mean . . . you got lost?' he frowned heavily, somewhat taken aback.

'Exactly what I said! I got lost! L-O-S-T!' she spelt out for him insolently. 'As in lost my way!'

Race looked as if he didn't know whether to believe her or not. 'How the hell could you?' he expostulated. 'The road's easy enough to follow.'

'Maybe it is . . . in daytime,' she allowed, piqued. 'But at night it's hard to tell which track leads where, and it doesn't help in the slightest with all those damned gates looking the same! Why don't you put signs on them, or something?'

'My God!' His eyes rolled skywards and then he began to laugh, mirthlessly. 'And to think Grant is proposing to have you aboard when he really heads off the beaten track! He must be crazy!' He abruptly fixed her with a shrewd look. 'Or doesn't he know your navigational abilities are exactly zero without a street directory?'

'They are not!' Kylie was forced into defending herself hotly. 'I did at least manage to find my own way back. And in any case, Grant's the navigator, I just do the driving.'

'Perhaps it's just as well, otherwise with you at the helm the pair of you might disappear into the mulga, never to be seen again,' Race drawled sarcastically.

'Which I've no doubt you would consider a fitting and welcome end where I'm concerned!'

'You sound very sure of that.' His shapely mouth took on a humorous curve.

'Why wouldn't I be?' she half laughed unsteadily. That smile of his was laying waste her defences. 'You make it all too obvious that anything which rid you of my unwanted presence would find favour in your eyes.'

'You would prefer it if I didn't make it obvious?'

'Oh, that's right, make fun of it!' Kylie tried to direct her wayward emotions to anger at his chaffing query. 'I should have known you'd find it amusing!'

'Amusing?' he repeated wryly and, to her amazement, with what appeared to be a thread of self-mockery in his tone. 'No, I don't find it amusing, sweetheart. Whenever you're involved I'd be more inclined to call it damned disturbing! And especially when I continually find myself experiencing a compulsive desire to do this!'

'This' was a sensuous attack on her already shaken senses as his firm mouth covered hers possessively, and his adroit left hand slid swiftly upwards from her arm to cradle the back of her head. Taken completely unawares by his action, Kylie's first unconscious reflex was to melt against him pliantly, her lips returning the ardent pressure with uninhibited fervour. Race had the power to affect her emotionally more than anyone she had ever known. But when reality finally began to intervene she desperately sought to restrain her turbulent feelings and wrenched her head away from the mind-drugging contact sharply.

'Don't!' she half ordered, half begged, huskily.

'Why not?' Darkened green eyes stared hypnotically into disturbed tawny-gold. 'It seems to be the only area where we're in accord.'

It wasn't a point Kylie could truthfully dispute and, moistening her lips nervously, she took an unsteady step backwards—to dismayingly discover the wall directly behind her. It made her feel trapped, both by his overwhelming presence and her own unruly emotions, and her breathing began to quicken agitatedly.

'That's h-hardly any reason to c-continue, though, is it?' she stammered.

Race leisurely outlined her softly trembling lower lip with a gentle forefinger. 'I can't think of any better.'

Kylie looked upward helplessly, wishing she could move away, but her feet seemed glued to the floor. 'Now I know you're making fun of me,' she accused tremulously, anguishedly.

'Then if I am, I'm making fun of myself too,' he murmured, and this time it was his lips which brushed tantalisingly across her mouth.

Before she could answer, even had she known what to say, Race had kissed her three times more. The length of contact increasing on each occasion until at last it was Kylie who, with almost a sob of wretchedness for not having been able to remain unmoved, ensured that the arousing encounter was kept constant by tangling her fingers within his hair and holding his head firmly in one place.

It was the first time in her life that she had ever made an active move to prolong or encourage any man's lovemaking, and although the reason escaped her as to why she should have chosen this man in particular to start on, it was apparent that Race had no complaints, because she was immediately swept closer to his sinewed frame by a securing arm which kept her pinned to the unhindered side of his broad chest.

Gradually, Kylie's fingers slipped from his head to trail savouringly over heavily muscled shoulders, unconsciously imagining the virile strength they presaged, and unaccountably she found herself wondering what it would be like to be held by both those powerful arms. Seconds later her thoughts were despatched to oblivion as Race's lips began to fire a relishing path of their own across a warmly flushed cheek to the lobe of her ear, and down the vulnerable arch of her throat to the furiously beating pulse in the hollow at its base.

'Dear God, I didn't realise the half of it when I said you were disturbing, did I, tiger eyes?' he charged ruefully when he eventually raised his head to look down at her slightly bemused features with a shadowed gaze.

'I'm sorry, that must be very annoying for you,' she apologised stiffly, a pretended impassivity her only barrier against the onslaught of feeling he had so effortlessly created. 'But I did ask you to stop, if you remember.'

'Do you regret that I didn't?'

'Yes!' How could she not when she was still trying to recover from the effects?

'Somehow that wasn't quite the impression *I* received,' Race smiled wryly.

Kylie's face burned. 'I—I wasn't anticipating it, that's all!'

A sardonically arched brow spoke volumes. 'You always respond so wholeheartedly when you're kissed without warning?' he quizzed.

'What else would you expect from someone with the morals of an alley cat?' she parried bitterly.

'You've certainly got the claws of one.'

The lazy drawl came as a surprise when she had been expecting instant agreement, and as a result the little control she had managed to salvage began to disappear again.

'Oh, stop it, Race!' She shook her head fretfully and sent him a bewildered gaze. 'I don't even know why you're doing this.'

His eyes held hers steadily. 'Perhaps I figured it was time we had a showdown.'

'Another one?' she half laughed brokenly.

'Let's hope, the last.'

'I see.' Her head drooped forward despondently. 'In other words, you can't wait the three weeks, or whatever, until I leave with Grant. You've come up with a new way for getting rid of me right now, is that it?'

'No, that is not it,' he denied, and tilted her face up to his again with a forceful hand. 'Or were you of the opinion I was kissing you goodbye just then?'

'I don't know,' she shrugged, her voice a throaty whisper. 'You could have been. You said you wanted a showdown, and—and that usually implies the finish of something.'

'So you automatically assumed I meant your presence, did you?'

Kylie moved restlessly from one foot to the other. 'It seemed the most logical explanation.'

'It didn't occur to you that I might have been suing for peace?' Race let go of her chin in order to slap his hand against a hard, muscled thigh in wry exasperation.

'Were you?' she countered, partly hopeful, but mostly apprehensive. The prospect may have been pleasing in one regard, but might not an unhostile Race Brandon be just a little too much to withstand?

'It seems like it.' And she wondered from his tone if he wasn't as surprised by the admission as she was. 'Although you sound as if you may have reservations about the idea.'

'Oh, no, not really,' she hastened into assuring him.

'Not really?' he proved intently.

'An—er—unthinking choice of words, nothing more,' she evaded.

'Kylie!' It was softly voiced, but it was a warning nonetheless.

'I think that's the first time you've ever used my right name,' she attempted to keep his attention diverted all the same.

'And I still think tiger eyes suits you better.' White teeth gleamed in a knowing smile as if he was supremely aware of what she was about. 'But you haven't explained yet. Not really . . .?' he prompted again.

Disconcerted by that look, Kylie hunched one shoulder selfconsciously and said hesitantly, 'I—well, it all depends on what you're intending to replace the antagonism with, doesn't it?'

'I guess it does, at that,' Race laughed drily. 'We'll just have to wait and see what ensues, won't we? But in the meantime . . .'

'Yes?' Amber eyes widened warily.

'The next time you plan on visiting my home while I'm away, how about your check with me first, not Grant, huh?'

As colour suffused her cheeks Kylie dropped her gaze to the middle of his chest. 'I'm sorry,' she murmured uncomfortably. Then her eyes flicked up to his again, anxiously. 'I didn't just invite myself over there, though. Adrian did ask me.'

'Mmm, so I heard . . . for tennis.'

A certain nuance in his voice had two deepening creases furrowing her forehead. 'You sound somehow . . . disbelieving.'

'Disappointed, would probably be more like it,' he returned blandly. 'At his lack of ingenuity.'

'I don't think I . . .,' she began in puzzlement, and then realisation came. 'Oh, no, there was nothing like that behind his invitation,' she hurried to convince him of Adrian's purely platonic friendship, although she couldn't really have said why it should be so important that she do so. 'It's just that I happened to mention at the sale that I'd like some practice before I played on Sunday and, as there aren't any courts here, he suggested I go over to Elouera Springs, that's all.' Pausing for a moment, she shrugged diffidently. 'As a matter of fact, I've arranged to go over there tomorrow afternoon as well . . . if that's all right with you, of course.'

'If I agree, are you sure you'll be able to find your way back here again okay?' he questioned banteringly, his eyes alive with such lazy laughter that Kylie had to swallow hard before she could answer.

'I—I'll make certain next time by leaving earlier. It was only when night fell that I had any difficulty.'

His head angled to one side speculatively. 'You're taking this all very seriously, aren't you?'

'What, the tennis?' she surmised. 'Well, I haven't played for some time now and I wouldn't like to let Adrian down too badly, seeing it's a round of the Club Championships.'

'But it is still only meant to be, more or less, a social game. I shouldn't let what Selena had to say the other night worry you too much, if I were you.'

'I'll try not to,' she smiled weakly, discomfitedly. She would have liked to have told him just how well she could play, but, wary of his reaction since Selena was concerned—she still wasn't sure yet just what relationship there existed between them—all she could do was drop hints. 'However, we do hope to make a slightly decent game of it. I mean, I expect even Selena and her partner would gain more satisfaction if we put up some sort of fight, rather than none at all.'

'Mmm, Brian might, but I don't know about Selena,'

he advised wryly. 'I rather think a six/nil result is the ultimate in her estimation.'

'Yes, well, I suppose it is in a way,' she conceded. 'But hardly what you would call challenging, all the same.'

'Exactly!'

'I see what you mean,' Kylie grinned crookedly. 'Selena doesn't want anyone else even venturing close to the top rung of *her* ladder.'

'That's about it,' he concurred, and draping a loose arm about her shoulders began leading her towards the hallway.

'A position by all accounts not totally undeserved, however,' she mused, sending him a measuring glance from beneath the cover of silky dark lashes. 'But as you've apparently been her partner in the mixed doubles for some years now, I guess you, more than anyone, would be aware of any—er—deficiencies in her game, wouldn't you?'

He nodded affirmatively. 'You could say that.'

When nothing else was forthcoming Kylie grimaced ruefully, then found herself on the receiving end of a very astute, very green gaze.

'You're not, by any chance, suggesting I should give you ideas as to the best way to defeat my former partner, are you?' he quizzed.

Of course she was! By the sound of it Adrian and herself would need all the help they could get. 'Would you . . . if I were?' she countered carefully.

His eyes roamed slowly, enigmatically over her upturned features. 'I might,' he raised her hopes, then promptly dashed them again by adding the qualification, '*if* I thought you needed any. Besides, haven't you already discussed all this with Adrian?'

'A little,' she admitted. 'But knowing Brian has a pretty fair all-round game, and that Selena's a hard hitter of the ball, even if she isn't terribly fast around the court, doesn't really give you much to go on.'

'So what are your and Adrian's weaknesses?'

'Ours?' She made a rueful moue. 'Probably too numerous to mention. For a start, we've never played together. Two, I'm horribly out of practice, and today I'm positive more of my serves went into the net than over it.' Maybe Selena had put a jinx on her in that regard with her talk at the table the other night! 'And three, my timing on overheads was decidedly suspect. Would you like me to continue?' Her mouth curved sardonically.

'You haven't mentioned any of Adrian's faults yet,' he reminded her.

'No? Well, perhaps I considered I had enough for both of us,' she returned mockingly. 'He reckons he usually makes a lot of unforced errors on his backhand volleys, but he seemed to be hitting them well enough today. Although I wasn't the only one experiencing difficulty with smashes. So you see,' she eyed him hopefully, even a little cajolingly, 'we *do* need help from whatever quarter we can find it.'

With a low, indulgent laugh which turned her bones to liquid, Race came to a halt and stood looking down at her, shaking his head wryly. 'I'm not quite sure why I should—except that I must be going soft in the head— but okay, I'll give you one tip regarding each of them. But no more, understood?'

Kylie assumed her most demure expression and nodded co-operatively.

'Hmm, I wish I knew how to get a result like that all

the time,' he owned in such an ironic drawl that she couldn't suppress a smile. Returning to the subject, he went on, 'With regard to Selena, you'll find she doesn't particularly care for lobs, and if they also happen to have some top spin on them she doesn't handle them very well either.'

'And Brian?' she urged, in case he had forgotten.

His mouth took on an oblique tilt. 'Don't panic, I was coming to that. In his case, I think the best advice I can give you is to watch his service. I don't know whether he realises or not—or even if anyone else has noticed—but he seems to serve in a pattern.'

'In what way?' she questioned immediately.

'If you kept quiet long enough, you might find out!' came the long-suffering retort.

'Sorry.' She schooled her features to meekness once more.

Race muttered something beneath his breath and continued. 'By pattern, I mean he almost invariably serves in threes. On his first three services he'll try across court towards the sideline, then for the next three he'll try down the centre line, and so on. I suspect it's only a subconscious rhythm he's got himself into, but that split second you save by knowing beforehand where he's going to aim his service can come in extremely handy at times.'

Wouldn't it, though! 'But surely Selena, at least, must have noticed what he's doing?'

'Apparently not,' he shrugged indifferently.

'And you're not going to tell her?'

'Uh-uh!' He shook his head slowly, an unabashed grin tugging at his lips. '*I* usually play against Brian, not with him.'

'In other words, charity starts at home,' Kylie laughed irrepressibly.

'Oh, indubitably!'

Ahead of them a face peered out from the kitchen. 'I thought I heard voices,' Abby smiled. And to Kylie, 'Have you just arrived back, love?'

'Mmm, not long since,' she confirmed selfconsciously, remembering all that had happened in the meantime as she and Race began moving again. 'I'm sorry I couldn't let you know I wouldn't make it for dinner, but . . .' she half smiled even more embarrassedly now, 'I somehow managed to get myself lost for a while on the way home.'

'Oh, dear, that must have been worrying for you at the time, but at least you made it safe and sound. You wouldn't have had anything to eat, then, at all, I suppose?' Fortunately, Abby was more concerned with the consequences of the incident rather than the causes.

Kylie moved one shoulder in a self-effacing movement. 'Mrs Hirst was kind enough to make some savouries for me before I left, but . . .'

'Then you'd better come and have something straight away. You must be starving by now,' deduced the blonde-haired woman.

'I wouldn't want to put you to any trouble,' diffidently.

'Good heavens, it's no trouble!' Abby discounted that idea with a laugh and pushed the kitchen door wider. 'Come on in, and I'll make you a cup of tea while I'm getting it ready.'

'Thank you,' smiled Kylie gratefully, beginning to follow her. After a couple of steps she looked back enquiringly to see if Race meant to join them, and found him almost directly behind her.

'It's not the first time Abby and I have had an evening chat around the kitchen table,' he answered her silent question with a smile. 'And especially since Sonia moved into a flat in town.'

'Sonia?' Her brows peaked in query.

'My daughter,' enlightened Abby over her shoulder as she set about filling the kettle. 'She turned eighteen earlier this year and now that she's got a job in town it's more convenient for her to live there than to keep travelling back and forth each day.'

If anything, Kylie's brows reached even higher. 'You've got an eighteen-year-old daughter!' she couldn't help exclaiming, astounded. She wouldn't have thought Abby was old enough to have a child of that age. In fact, it had never even occurred to her that Abby might have been married at one time. There were certainly no rings in evidence on her fingers.

'That she has,' corroborated Race, holding out a chair for Kylie at the table before turning one around for himself and straddling it. 'An exact replica of her mother too, I might add. Blonde, blue-eyed, and extremely hard to get the better of in an argument,' he laughed across at the older woman.

'Don't give me that, Race Brandon! I've never won an argument with you yet,' Abby immediately fired back with an answering chuckle. Kylie wondered if anyone ever had, except maybe Grant. Race just didn't give the impression that he was accustomed to losing, at anything! 'As for Sonia,' Abby continued, 'well, maybe it's not a bad thing that she isn't afraid to say what she thinks. Perhaps if I'd been as outspoken at her age I wouldn't have taken quite so much for granted, and then found myself in the unenviable position I did. It's only since Grant took us in that I've gained enough confidence in my own judgment not to unquestioningly believe whatever I'm told.'

'Mmm, you didn't have much to say for yourself when you first arrived, did you?' Race recalled humorously, eyes dancing. A gleaming white smile swept his curving lips upwards and had Kylie looking elsewhere in an effort to nullify its effect on her nervous system. 'It's a pity some things can't always stay the same, isn't it?' he teased.

'I'll say!' Abby was all too willing to jokingly agree. 'In those days you were only my employer's young nephew, now you're my *boss*! My God, the depths I've sunk to!' she taunted in mock despair.

It was clear that this kind of exchange was nothing new to either of them and Kylie started to laugh at the housekeeper's melodramatic expression.

'Just how long have you worked here, Abby?' she queried, still smiling.

'Seventeen and a half years,' the other woman revealed with a shake of her head and a click of her tongue as if amazed at the rapid passing of time. 'Sonia was still just a baby when I wrote in answer to Grant's advertisement for a housekeeper. It was the last resort for me. You see, I—I was . . .' She looked to Race, almost as if for guidance, then shrugged and apparently made her own decision. 'It's no secret, so I guess I may as well be the one to tell you, but I was—am—an unmarried mother. Only then it wasn't so usual for girls to keep the children they bore out of wedlock, and neither, unfortunately, were people so tolerant of those who did,' she sighed regretfully, all traces of amusement gone now. 'As I said, Grant was my last resort. I'd been refused so many positions on account of Sonia that I was at my wits' end. Even my own parents had disowned me. But luckily for me, Grant was more understanding. He gave me the job because he knew how desperately I needed it, even though there were others who applied with better qualifications than mine, and for that I owe him a debt of gratitude I can never repay. He's been a surrogate father to Sonia, a helpful adviser and confidant to me, and a considerate employer. There wasn't anything else I could have asked of the man, so you'll have to excuse me at times if I seem somewhat one-eyed where he's concerned because, to my mind, he can do no wrong.' Pausing, she gave an apologetic grin for her vehemence and, seeking to return to a less solemn atmosphere, remarked brightly, 'And now, that I've got that off my chest, what would you like to eat? Steak and vegetables, cold meat and salad, an omelette perhaps?'

'Oh—er—cold meat and salad will do, thanks, Abby,' Kylie stammered, the question catching her unawares. Her thoughts were still surrounding a young girl with a baby to feed and care for seventeen years ago. No wonder Abby thought so much of Grant. Who wouldn't after being rescued from such dire straits?

A large teapot was placed on the table along with some cups and saucers, and a pair of blue eyes suddenly intercepted Kylie's line of vision.

'I haven't shocked you, have I?' Abby half smiled, half frowned. 'You've gone very quiet.'

'No, of course you haven't shocked me,' she denied earnestly, and a little discomfited to find herself the subject for two green eyes now, as well as the blue. 'I was just thinking how typical that would be of Grant. He really is a very thoughtful and understanding person, and it never ceases to amaze me that some woman didn't snap him up years ago.'

'Maybe he just preferred to remain unshackled,' put in Race dampeningly.

'And maybe the right woman just didn't happen along either,' countered Abby determinedly. 'Not everyone takes quite such a negative view of marriage as you do, you know. Besides,' her eyes twinkled roguishly, 'even though you've been determined to avoid it so far, that still doesn't mean you won't go the way of all good men some time in the not too distant future.'

Race's reply to that prediction was a burst of highly amused laughter, followed by a challenging, 'You wouldn't care to lay out any money on that, would you?'

Abby merely smiled in a superior fashion and returned her attention to other matters, leaving Kylie to muse over what had been said with a decidedly empty feeling in her stomach, but which she put down to the fact that it had been so long since she'd last eaten. After all, why would it matter to her, one way or the other, whether Race married or not?

CHAPTER SEVEN

SUNDAY was a beautiful day with only a few traces of cloud in the sky, hardly any breeze, and pleasantly warm without being too hot. Just perfect for tennis, in fact, as testified by the number of people who arrived at Elouera Springs for a game. It seemed to Kylie that the whole district had turned out for the day, and as the Championship rounds had been set down for the afternoon and the morning reserved for purely social games, she offered her services to Mrs Hirst in case an extra pair of hands was needed to help with the luncheon arrangements.

There were quite a few of the other women in the large kitchen when she arrived, and although she had been introduced to most of them at one time or another during the morning it took a while before she became familiar with each of their names—except for Abby and her daughter Sonia, whose features were truly a duplicate of her mother's and therefore easy to remember.

It was to be a basket lunch, Kylie found, where everyone had brought along a selection of food which was then all laid out together on tables beneath the trees, smorgasbord-style, so that they could all help themselves to whatever they fancied. In the kitchen it was just a matter of taking the prepared food out of the various containers it had arrived in and arranging it on plates which would then be taken outside at the appropriate time, as well as making up jugs of icy cold drinks and being certain there was enough water on the boil to fill the extremely large pots to be used for the tea. Not surprisingly, there was a good deal of talk and laughter around the table, together with varying comments as the individual offerings were revealed, and although lack of local knowledge prevented Kylie from participating in some of their conversations, it was obvious that they were trying to keep those subjects to a minimum in order that she didn't feel excluded.

Soon, however, it was time for the food to be taken outside, and it was on the first of her trips from the kitchen that Kylie noticed Selena—who had been conspicuous by her absence inside—sitting with some friends around a lacy wrought iron table close to the verandah steps, and shaded by a colourfully patterned umbrella.

'Oh, there you are, Kylie,' the statuesque girl called out in feigned surprise. 'I was wondering where you were hiding. I thought you might have had second thoughts about partnering Adrian in the doubles this afternoon.'

'No, no second thoughts. I'm still available,' Kylie smiled back sweetly. 'That is . . . provided *you're* still as keen to play *us*, of course.'

Selena could hardly contain her smug laughter. 'I'm so glad you have a sense of humour,' she sniggered. 'It will serve you in good stead for after our match. We're scheduled as the first game after lunch, you know.'

'Mmm, so Adrian informed me earlier. I shall have to watch I don't eat too much, won't I?'

'Do you think it will make any difference?' Selena's superciliousness was less concealed now.

'Kylie shrugged artlessly. 'Who can tell? But it might

be the difference between winning and losing.'

'A game, I presume you mean.'

'A game, a set, the match.' Kylie shrugged again. 'I wouldn't like to say.'

'Well, I would,' retorted Selena with overweening confidence. 'Because I doubt very much if you and Adrian will even win a set, let alone the match.'

Slow footsteps sounded on the path behind them as Mrs Hirst went ambling by with a plate in each hand. 'There's many a slip "twixt cup and lip", she muttered, seemingly to herself, as she continued on her way.

Kylie hid a grin as best she could, but Selena's eyes followed the slightly stooped figure of the housekeeper with a malevolent look. 'That old witch should have been turned off this place years ago!' she hissed. 'Useless old crone!'

'Who, Mrs Hirst?' asked one of her companions, eyebrows lifting.

'Who else?' Selena almost spat in return.

'Oh, I don't know, she's a bit on the slow side, I grant you, but otherwise she's okay. At least, she always has been to me,' the other girl replied.

'Well, she hasn't to me . . . as you just heard!'

'But that's just her way. You're taking her too personally. In any case, what she said is quite true. You shouldn't count your chickens before they're hatched.' She looked to Kylie with a friendly smile, querying, 'Should she?'

'Oh, spare me the quaint little proverbs, Evelyn, for heaven's sake!' retorted Selena in a disgruntled tone, and only giving Kylie the opportunity to return the seated girl's smile noncommitally. 'You know as well as I damned well do who's going to win that doubles match, and counting chickens and all the rest of it isn't going to alter the outcome one iota! As for Mrs Hirst— well, you can believe what you want to, but if I had my way I'd have her off this property so fast her feet wouldn't touch the ground!'

Realising the futility of the discussion, Evelyn merely gave a ruefully resigned shake of her head, and Kylie headed towards the tables after the housekeeper. So far she could only second Evelyn's opinion. Mrs Hirst had never said anything exceptional to her. And perhaps, she surmised, if Selena had treated the woman with a little more tolerance she might have been able to say the same too.

Mrs Hirst had just arranged her plates on one of the tables when Kylie arrived, and she turned to the younger girl with a frowning look creasing her forehead into even deeper lines than usual.

'Don't you pay any attention to Miss High-and-Mighty's boasting, you hear? She's not that good that she can't be beaten, so you go out there and do your best, young Kylie!'

She made it sound like an order and Kylie nodded her agreement willingly. 'I'll certainly try, Mrs Hirst,' she smiled. 'And thank you for the encouragement. From the way Selena was talking I think we'll need every bit we can get.'

'Hah! That's just what she wants you to think. But you forget, I've seen you play. In fact, except for Adrian, I'm probably the only one who has, and you're no novice at the game, that I do know, my girl,' Mrs Hirst chuckled with patent delight, her pale blue eyes lighting pleasurably. 'If the two of you play as well as you did that last afternoon you were here, you'll have a

very good chance of winning. The only way you'd have
a better one was if Race partnered you. Hmm . . .' she
let out her breath disappointedly, 'it's a pity he's
strapped up like he is. You and he would make a fine
pair.'

Although she was finding it an unaccountably pleasant thought to contemplate, Kylie still felt she had to
remind her, 'But if he wasn't injured he—he'd . . .' She
came to a selfconscious halt as the subject of their discussion suddenly appeared beside them.

'Yes, yes? He'd . . . what?' demanded Mrs Hirst unperturbed.

With a strain of colour climbing her cheeks Kylie
finally took the opportunity to put her own plates on
the table. 'He'd be partnering Selena, as usual,' she
mumbled.

Mrs Hirst cupped a hand to her ear. 'Eh? What was
that?' Then immediately she questioned of Race, 'What
did she say?'

Bending closer to her ear, his eyes never leaving
Kylie's averted face, he repeated, 'She said, "He would
be partnering Selena, as usual".'

'Oh, yes, I suppose so. A pity.' His housekeeper
sounded crestfallen.

'Why's that?' probed Race interestedly. It was obvious from his expression that he was all too aware just
who "he" was.

'Because I think you and young Kylie here would
make an unbeatable combination,' she had no hesitation in informing him.

'But neither have Selena and I been beaten yet.'

'Ah! But you haven't seen this one play!' Mrs Hirst
all but crowed triumphantly.

'Oh?' speculatively. 'I was under the impression Kylie was strictly one of the hit-and-miss type.'

'Were you now?' chortled Mrs Hirst, really getting into her stride. 'Then you're going to be in for a shock this afternoon, aren't you?'

On seeing Abby and Sonia pass by loaded down with food, Kylie decided now was as good a time as any to make her exit. Before Mrs Hirst could unwittingly spill any more beans! Smiling weakly, she took a couple of hasty steps backward. 'If you'll excuse me, I think I'd better get back and help the others.'

'And I think not, tiger eyes!' Race's hand descended on to the back of her neck before she could take a third step. '*I* think you've got some explaining to do first.'

'A-about what?'

'The reason you found it necessary to apparently underrate your ability will do for a beginning!'

'I didn't! It was Selena who suggested I couldn't play,' she muttered defiantly. 'I just went along with it.'

'In your normal fashion!'

'That's right, in my normal fashion,' she concurred flippantly. 'So why should you care?'

From the look on his face Kylie was positive he would have shaken her furiously if they hadn't been in view of so many people, and she shivered involuntarily.

'I'll tell you why I care!' he gritted between clenched teeth. 'Firstly, because I don't like being sweet-talked into giving away the weaknesses in other people's games by someone sailing under false colours! And secondly, just how do you think I feel after I've spent most of the morning with Brian trying to persuade him not to take it too hard on you because you're not a very experienced player.?'

Golden brown eyes stared upwards incredulously. 'You did that . . . for me?'

'No, for Adrian,' Race squashed the suggestion savagely. 'I thought, by the sound of it, he'd be taking on the pair of them more or less on his own.'

'I see.' Kylie blinked rapidly at the sudden onrush of dampness in her eyes, her head drooping dejectedly.

This time the hand on her neck did shake her, but not nearly so violently as she had previously envisaged. 'Oh, for God's sake, of course it was for you!' he admitted in roughened tones. 'I've seen Adrian beaten too many times before to start worrying about it now.'

'Then, thank you,' she smiled tremulously. 'And— and I'm sorry if it's put you in an embarrassing position with regard to Brian. Perhaps you could tell him it was all a mistake.'

'From what Mrs H. had to say, I'm sure he's going to realise that very smartly once you're all on the court,' he replied drily.

Still unashamedly listening to all that was being said, his housekeeper nodded her agreement with undisguised enthusiasm.

'Yes, but . . .'

'Don't worry about it,' he recommended with a negligent lift of one shoulder. 'Even if Brian had planned to take it easy, you can be very certain he didn't intend taking it to the stage where there was a chance you might win. He's not *that* obliging!'

'I still wouldn't like him to think you'd deliberately misled him.'

Race shook his head unconcernedly. 'He won't. I've no doubt Selena's already convinced him much the same. In any case, isn't psychology the name of the game in most sports these days?' The corners of his firmly moulded mouth quirked indolently. 'Especially the element of surprise ... as you're obviously well aware.'

'And isn't it going to give a couple of people a surprise?' interposed Mrs Hirst, unable to keep silent any longer. 'I don't usually watch many of the Club's matches, but this one I definitely won't be missing!'

'With no prize for guessing which team you'll be supporting either,' said Race in a wry voice.

'Well, you wouldn't expect me to cheer for *that* one, would you?' she returned somewhat testily, and leaving none of them in any doubt as to whom she meant. She sent her employer a sly, assessing glance. 'And unless I miss my guess, you'll be on the same side as I am too!'

As much as Kylie would have liked to have believed Mrs Hirst's assumption she couldn't quite bring herself to, and she waited for Race to confirm or deny it in a suspended state of part hope, and part disbelief.

'Mmm, I suppose it would only be right to support the two who are in the family's employ, wouldn't it?' he mused. 'And it is the national trait to cheer for the underdog.'

'That's as may be,' snorted his housekeeper in disgust, even as Kylie's hopes took a plunge. Somehow— foolishly, it seemed—she had persuaded herself it may have been for reasons other than the two mentioned. 'But it has no bearing whatsoever on this particular contest.'

'You think not?' With a grin he still refused to give her a definite answer.

'Bah! You're wasting my time, and you always did

try my patience when you started bandying words! If you were honest with yourself you'd admit it!' she snapped irascibly before storming off as rapidly as someone of her advanced years could in righteous indignation.

Race watched her departure with traces of a smile hovering on his lips. 'At least you always know where you are with Mrs H. She say's exactly what's on her mind.'

'You don't think you should go after her?' Kylie suggested worriedly. 'She seemed quite upset.'

An impenitent laugh issued from the strong column of his throat. 'Only because she couldn't get the answer she wanted.'

'Because she was wrong?' Kylie chewed at her lip dismally.

'Is that what you think?'

She nodded mutely.

Warm fingers slid tantalisingly along the side of her jaw to her chin, tilting her pensive features up to his. 'Then I suggest you revise your thinking, sweetheart,' he drawled softly.

Tawny eyes searched darkened green ones wonderingly. 'You mean . . .?'

'I've cruelly deserted my former partner and transferred my allegiance elsewhere for the match?' He nodded decisively. 'Yes.'

'Because we both work for Brandons, and we're also the underdogs?'

Race removed his fingers from her chin in order to rake them through his darkly curling hair. 'Oh, hell, you really want the last drop of blood, don't you?' he signed in a kind of ironic exasperation.

'Do I?' Kylie frowned, uncomprehending.

'Apparently,' he endorsed, his expression altering to one of slightly mocking amusement.

Thinking the mockery directed at herself, Kylie stiffened. 'Then I'm sorry. It wasn't intentional.'

'It probably wasn't,' he laughed shortly. 'But unfortunately that doesn't happen to alter anything, sweetheart. You've still managed to get under my skin, and even though I may not be particularly enamoured with the situation, at the moment there doesn't seem to be a damned thing I can do about it!'

Kylie stared at him in astonishment. The idea that he might have been as unsettled by her presence as she was by his—even unwillingly—just hadn't figured within her realms of possibilities. Those times he had kissed her she had attributed to a wish to merely prove how vulnerable her emotions were, certainly not an attraction, however reluctant, on his part.

But now that she knew differently, an unbidden tremor of excitement coursed through her as she realised how much she had been secretly longing for just such a happening—a shiver which was quickly tempered by a reflex wariness. When he said she had managed to get under his skin, he could of course have been likening her to a splinter. Something to be removed and disposed of as soon as possible!

As a result, her next words were tinged with more than a little selfconsciousness as she lifted one slender shoulder and apologised diffidently, 'I'm sorry. I guess, one way or another, I've been something of a problem ever since I arrived, haven't I?'

What his comments might have been on that theory Kylie never heard, because Adrian forestalled his reply by choosing that moment to join them.

'Hi! All set for this afternoon?' he asked her with a bracing smile.

'I will be, as soon as I've finished helping bring the food out and lunch is over,' she answered, and deciding it was probably a prudent time, prepared to leave.

'Oh, great!' Adrian's mouth curved wryly in disappointment. 'The minute I turn up, you depart. You're not trying to tell me something, are you?'

'With Kylie, who would know?' inserted Race whimsically, and perhaps a little sardonically, to Kylie's mind. 'I think she likes to keep us all guessing by disconcertingly saying—and doing—the exact opposite to what everyone expects.'

'Oh?' His manager's fair brows lifted slightly, puzzledly.

'Only when circumstances dictate,' Kylie countered Race's suggestion a trifle tauntingly. She turned to Adrian to urge, 'Pay no attention to him. Nothing was further from my mind in this instance. It's just that I feel guilty for not lending more of a hand.' Eyeing the increasing number of plates arriving on the table, she smiled excusingly. 'I really should go. Perhaps we could talk during lunch instead?' she offered.

'You're on!' he agreed readily. 'I'll keep a place for you under the tree over there,' indicating some seats which had been set up a short distance away from the tables.

For some indefinable reason her eyes sought Race, as if seeking approval before complying, and found him watching her lazily.

'That's where we normally sit,' he advised with an

unencouraging shrug.

'I—well—I'll see you there, then,' she faltered, including them both in her uncertain half smile, and made good her departure without giving either of them a chance to say anything further. Right at the moment she had enough to think about, what with Race's totally unexpected admission, and all!

As it was, Kylie was unable to say much at all to Adrian during lunch as a space had been reserved for her between Race and Grant—with a rather overbearing Selena on her former partner's other side—and not next to the younger man as she had imagined would be the case.

Nevertheless, directly the meal was concluded, and a suitable time allowed for digestion, the two of them naturally gravitated together as they went to collect their racquets from the verandah. For Kylie, the same one she had borrowed on the two previous occasions, since she had never anticipated needing her own when she originally set out with Grant.

'Well, that didn't exactly work out the way I planned,' remarked Adrian drily once they had left the others behind.

'For me either,' Kylie laughed ruefully. It had been bad enough watching Selena commandeer almost the whole of Race's attention, without being prevented—by distance—from engaging in some small talk herself with someone her own age. At the same time, she didn't want him getting the wrong idea, and she added hurriedly, 'I could have done with some help occasionally to break up Grant and Victor's discussions on farming.' She gave a wry chuckle. 'Although, now I come to think of it, you would probably have joined in with them instead.'

'Not me,' he disputed adamantly. 'It's all things in order of importance as far as I'm concerned, and today, work is definitely *out*!'

Mounting the steps on to the verandah, Kylie picked up her racquet from where it had been resting on a table and began unzipping the cover. 'As long as that doesn't include work on the tennis court,' she teased.

'Not likely!' He shook his head, smiling, and testing the strings of his own racquet. 'This afternoon's going to be a do or die effort for me. I'll never have a better chance of getting into the next round, and I'm not likely to have such a good partner again either. No, it will be an all-out effort from me today, I can assure you.'

'The same here,' she promised.

Adrian swept an arm towards the steps. 'Then, if you're ready, shall we let battle commence?' he joked.

'May as well,' she acceded with a grimace, moving forward. 'Otherwise my nerves may yet get the better of me.'

Good lord! Why would someone who plays as well as you do be nervous?'

'Probably because I can't help it. It's an old habit of mine,' she laughed, making light of it. She didn't also add that knowing Race would be watching may have had something to do with it too!

'Never mind, you'll feel better once it's started, I expect,' he averred comfortingly as they began threading their way between the various groups preparing to watch the match. Then, seeing a middle-aged man dressed in white shorts and a red and white striped T-shirt take a seat beside the court and in line with net, he murmured in patent satisfaction, 'Ah, so Jimmy got the nod from the Committee as umpire, after all, did he?'

'I gather from your tone that that's good,' Kylie guessed, amused.

'Better than having Carmel Dodds, who was the other choice, that's for sure!'

'Why's that?'

'Because Carmel happens to be a very firm friend of Selena's and, whether intentionally or not, has been known to occasionally give Selena the benefit of the doubt when others have been of the opinion that the call should have gone against her,' he supplied satirically.

'Oh, nice!' she commented mockingly. 'And the lines . . . men? Women? Persons?'

He nodded towards a group of teenagers, Sonia among them, standing at the side of the court. 'The older kids,' he advised, grinning. 'They reckon they've got the best eyesight.'

'Mmm, they could have something there,' she conceded with an appreciative laugh. 'And do they also compete in the Championships?'

'My word, and very well too, I might add,' he confessed somewhat lugubriously. 'The singles finals will be no foregone conclusion this year. In fact, even in the doubles, everyone believes there's only young Sonia and her partner, Ivan Morphett, who have any show of deposing Selena and Brian.' He winked at her conspiratorially. 'Except that we mean to beat 'em to it.'

'If possible,' Kylie agreed, but on a cautious note. She still would have preferred to have seen the other pair play before making any rash forecasts.

Almost to the court's edge, Adrian directed her towards a small gathering occupying a bench seat, and

which included Race and his uncle, Mrs Hirst and
Victor, as well as their opponents and a few others.

'You certainly took your time getting here!' snapped
Selena in annoyance immediately they were within talking range. 'We've been waiting for at least ten minutes
for you.'

'Well, three,' corrected Mrs Hirst in a stage whisper,
and was rewarded by a dark-eyed glare of promised re-
tribution which she returned unflinchingly.

'Sorry,' Adrian apologised offhandedly, and took a
look at his watch. 'We've still got another five minutes
before we're due to start, though.'

'Quite possibly, but I would like a decent period for a
warm-up. That is, if you don't mind, of course!' Selena
heaved sarcastically.

'Not at all,' he shrugged. 'Kylie and I wouldn't say
no to that either.'

'No, I don't suppose you would,' she smirked meaningfully, and rose to her feet.

During the minor confrontation Kylie had purposely
kept her gaze downward, but as the others prepared to
move on to the court, she lifted it again and instinctively looked to Race.

As their glances connected his dark head inclined
slightly and he smiled indolently, a fascinatingly slow
curving of his firm mouth which—as ever—had her insides somersaulting uncontrollably.

'Good luck!' he offered in dry tones.

'Thank you,' shyly.

Turning away, she came face to face with an irate
Selena who had clearly overheard the exchange and was
now fixing her former partner with a furious stare. But
when he merely acknowledged her incensed look with a

challengingly raised eyebrow, she pulled herself up sharply and passed off his apparent defection with a short laugh.

'Oh, well, I guess they need all the luck they can get,' she belittled spitefully before turning on her heel and striding across to the umpire.

Kylie followed her rather more slowly—though no less determinedly—her previous nervousness dissipating swiftly as irritation at Selena's disparaging remark took its place, and even more resolved now than before to put a dent or two in the voluptuous brunette's insufferable ego.

The toss went to the older pair, with Selena electing to serve from that end of the court where the greater majority of the spectators had gathered. Just to make the ball that much harder to distinguish, deduced Kylie knowingly. She had played under these types of conditions before.

Their warm-up proceeded satisfactorily enough, except that each time Selena directed a ball towards Kylie she would loop it gently over the net as if that was the only shot the younger girl was able to return. Naturally enough, on seeing her actions the crowd automatically assumed the slender girl in the white scooped-neck top and pale lemon shorts wasn't a particularly competent player, but as far as Kylie herself was concerned the time for play-acting was past and she made her returns with all her normal smooth grace.

At last the game was about to get under way, but as Selena and Brian took up their places in readiness, Adrian hurried across to Kylie before she could reach the base line.

'Would you prefer it if I received first?' he questioned helpfully.

'What, from Selena? Uh-uh!' She shook her head vehemently. 'No, that first ball's *mine*!

'Okay, love, she's all yours,' he smiled understandingly, and headed for his own position closer towards the net.

The signal was given for the game to begin and Kylie adopted a loose-limbed half crouch, concentrating unwaveringly on the tall figure the other end as the ball was bounced three times and then tossed high into the air. Racquet and ball met with tremendous force—Selena wasn't pretending to take it easy any more!—and then Kylie was moving to her right. The hurtling ball had been aimed across the service court on to her forehand and she made for it confidently, sending it back over the net in a driving return which caught Selena completely unprepared and which passed her before she had even taken two steps forward.

Apparently, the server wasn't the only one to be taken by surprise either, for a momentary hush suddenly fell over those watching as they assimilated the rarity of Selena losing a point on the return of her service. The two men on the court weren't nearly so restrained, however, and let their feelings be known in no uncertain manner.

'You little beauty!' applauded Adrian, grinning broadly.

'Good grief! For someone who isn't supposed to play very well, she sure carved up your service, Selena,' groaned Brian, sounding stunned and, perhaps, just a little amused.

'A fluke!' his partner snarled, her expression rancorous. 'It won't happen again!'

Kylie kept her thoughts to herself, only permitting herself a small inward smile of satisfaction as she took up her new position.

From then on no one took anyone else lightly, and it soon became obvious to the crowd that they were watching the match of the season as both pairs fought valiantly for each and every point. But, fortunately for Kylie and Adrian, that first boomer of a return must have rattled Selena to her foundations, because she never quite recovered in that game, and the ensuing break of her service was sufficient to allow them to eventually take out the first set.

'So far, so good,' panted Adrian as they took a well-earned break and a couple of mouthfuls of drink.

'Mmm.' Kylie wiped beads of perspiration away from her temples with the back of her hand. 'But Selena will really be out for revenge in this next set. The match is the best of three, I presume?'

'It is, and you're right about the next set too. If they don't take it they're out of the doubles. For this year, at least.'

'Then we'll just have to make certain we win it, won't we?' she smiled mischievously.

'Poor Brian,' he could find it in his heart to sympathise with his opposite number. 'He's been wanting to win this title for years.'

'Yes, well, I am rather sorry he's become caught up in all of this. He seems like a good sport. Anyway,' she grimaced wryly, 'he might still win it. We're no certainties, even yet.'

'Unfortunately, you never spoke a truer word,' he admitted in kind. 'They're not giving an inch, are they?'

And neither did they in the second set, which was a

see-sawing affair, and which saw all four of them, at one time or another, lose their sevices—a circumstance that evened the score, and that was how it stayed until they reached six games all, and they went into a tie-breaker.

Now Selena and Brian began to apply a little strategy of their own, concentrating on Adrian to make him play all the shots and deliberately keeping their returns well out of Kylie's reach. For a time it was successful and they won four points in a row, until Kylie forced them to relinquish the ploy by covering Adrian so well that they lost the next three points.

That still left the younger pair one point behind, and knowing it was imperative they regain it as quickly as possible, Kylie purposely played a shorter ball for Selena during the next rally, bringing the other girl in to the net, and then lobbed the return high over her head. Even had Selena been faster on her feet it was clear from the time the ball began its descent that she wasn't going to reach it in time, and although Brian made a desperate effort to get across the court, he was still too late to do anything but watch as it landed just within the triangle created by the juncture of the side and base lines, and then bounce out of play.

They were all square once again and the battle for supremacy had to be re-started. But this time it was Kylie and Adrian who drew slightly ahead, and then, unbelievably, they only needed to take one more point and the match would be theirs. Breathing deeply to steady herself, Kylie prepared to serve to Brian, sending the ball into the far corner of the service court and then moving in swiftly to intercept his forehand return. It came on just the angle she had hoped and, with a hasty mental prayer, she took it on her backhand to execute a drop volley so that it cleared the net by only a matter of centimetres before losing its momentum and falling like a stone on the other side.

Selena made a wild dash forward, but the ball was already lying dead on the court before she scooped it up and into the net, while the spontaneous and prolonged applause from the spectators left no doubt in anyone's mind that the match was well and truly over.

Running the distance that separated them, Adrian dropped his racquet uncaringly in order to wrap his arms about Kylie in joyful exuberance and swing her off her feet.

'You did it! You're a bloody marvel!' he beamed jubilantly.

'I thought it was a combined effort,' she gasped, hardly able to breathe.

He lowered her to the ground gently, shaking his head. 'No, I may have played my best ever tennis, but that was only because I was being pulled along by you. My love, in case you don't know it, at times you have touches of absolute brilliance I could never even remotely approach,' he claimed fervently as he bent to retrieve his racquet and they went to meet their defeated opponents at the net.

'I disagree,' was the only rejection Kylie had time to make before shaking hands with Brian and thanking him for such a good game, while Adrian did the same with Selena.

'It was my pleasure,' Brian returned with a smile. 'We may not have won, but it was one of the most enjoyable games I've played in a long time. I like a close finish.'

An attitude his partner more than obviously didn't

share, from the look of livid fury evident on Selena's
features when Kylie held out a hand to her in turn. Just
managing to touch fingertips, she didn't even bother to
mention the game, but promptly hissed, 'All right, Miss
Smarty! I challenge you to a singles match! Then we'll
see who comes out on top!'

'Not today you won't. There isn't time,' broke in
Brian with an apologetic look at Kylie for the older
girl's behaviour.

'Then we'll make time! I'm the Secretary of this Club,
remember?'

'You still can't...'

'Don't you presume to tell me what I can or can't do,
Brian Antill!' she raged at him. 'If it wasn't for you I'd
still have a chance at the mixed doubles final! You
played atrociously!' Leaving them standing, she began
storming for the sideline.

A rueful grin edged its way on to Brian's lips as the
three of them started to follow her. 'To put it kindly, I
think Selena is a little sore at having lost,' he pro-
pounded drily.

'I think she's just a damned rotten sportswoman!' put
in Adrian bluntly.

'I'm inclined to agree,' added Kylie. 'After all, you
could say *she* lost you the first set by not holding her
service.'

'Hmm, I must remember that,' Brian nodded
thoughtfully, humorously. 'I wonder if that's how Race
manages to keep her in line when he's partnering her?
By continually reminding her that *her* game isn't exactly
perfect in every respect either.'

Mention of Race had Kylie looking ahead to see if he
was still with Grant and the others on the bench, and it

came as a painful shock to see him walking away from them towards the homestead with Selena by his side. Maybe the other girl had been right, she mused despondently. Maybe he had only wished them luck because he hadn't expected them to win, and now that they had, he was more concerned in offering his condolences to Selena than congratulations to Adrian and herself.

Not that there weren't sufficient people there who were ready to applaud them, as well as proferring words of sympathy to Brian, but although it was very warming, it wasn't the same somehow. It had been Race's comments—and, possibly, approval—she had been subconsciously seeking. With a sigh she slumped on to the seat beside Mrs Hirst, her racquet held loosely between her legs.

'What's Race doing ... consoling Selena?' she probed, her tone defensively flippant.

'Consoling her!' The housekeeper's lips turned down at the corners in disgust. 'I hope he's flaying her for the disgraceful exhibition she put on. How dared she speak to Brian like that!'

'You heard?' Kylie's eyes widened in amazement. If Mrs Hirst heard, then presumably so did everyone else!

'Of course we did! *That* one never bothers to keep her voice down when something's annoyed her. She was still complaining about him when she came through here.'

'Oh, that's not fair,' Kylie immediately defended the hapless Brian. 'I didn't think he played too badly.'

'Neither did anyone else,' came the succinct retort. 'The weakest link on that court was young Adrian, so I don't know what she's got to whine about.'

'Perhaps it was just the shock of losing. I mean, it was obvious she had never once even contemplated that they might not win.'

'Then it serves her right,' Mrs Hirst declared unsympathetically. 'No one is ever that good that they can't be beaten.'

'No, but she wasn't expecting me to play quite as well as I did, and . . .'

'Are you making excuses for her?' the housekeeper barked incredulously, and fixing her with a glare of piercing blue.

'No, of course not,' Kylie grimaced. 'Her behaviour *was* shocking. Only . . .'

'Yes?'

She shrugged uncomfortably. 'Only I feel guilty hearing her take out her disappointment on Brian, when it's really my fault for having led her into thinking I couldn't play,' she owned in a rush.

'And do you really think it would have made any difference if she had known, and you'd still beaten her?'

'I—I don't know.'

'Well, I do!' Mrs Hirst had no hesitation in exclaiming. 'I've known Selena Walmsley since she was born and, believe me, your having told her you could play well wouldn't have altered her attitude in the slightest when she lost. She's never been any different, and I don't suppose she ever will be. Pure and simply, she's just a bad loser!'

It was much the same as Adrian had said to Brian after the game, and she had been in accordance with his views then, so why was she letting it trouble her now? Because Race might think they had taken advantage of the other pair and that was why he was with Selena at the moment? To soothe her ruffled feelings at having lost due to a subterfuge?

Sighing, she allowed, 'I guess so,' in answer to the housekeeper's claim, and when that woman left to return to the homestead, watched unseeingly as another two couples took to the court for a game of doubles.

Her thoughts were still turned inward when a hand came to rest on her shoulder, making her jump visibly, and the warm voice which murmured close beside her right ear, 'Congratulations! That was some match you just played,' did nothing to ease the sudden pounding of her heart.

Kylie twisted around quickly, knowing that voice anywhere, and saw Race resting easily on his haunches just behind her, the slope of the land making his head the higher.

'Where's Adrian?' he questioned amiably. 'I thought he'd still be with you.'

'No, he's down there somewhere.' She nodded to farther along the bench.

'Lapping up the plaudits, I suppose?'

Her golden brown eyes became wary. 'Don't you think he's entitled to?'

'Not particularly.' He shook his head slowly, his thickly lashed eyes never wavering from hers.

'I see,' she acknowledged faintly, even white teeth beginning to worry at her bottom lip.

'That's good,' he declared in sardonic tones. 'Because I don't.'

'I'm sorry?' she frowned her bewilderment.

'I don't see the reason for your sudden withdrawal just because I happen to think Adrian left you to do too much work out there,' he elucidated tautly.

'You mean, it wasn't because you were annoyed at the—er——' she hunched one shoulder awkwardly, her gaze dropping to his sling-encased arm, 'at the circumstances surrounding our win?'

The hand on her shoulder moved slightly to cover the nape of her neck, his thumb sliding smoothly up and down the satiny skin. 'I understood those were created by skilful play.'

'No, the other,' she reminded him throatily.

Sweetheart, after you hit that first ball, there *were* no others,' he laughed wryly. 'If that didn't give them fair warning of what to expect, then nothing would.'

Unable to completely shed the feeling of guilt which assailed her, Kylie stated the obvious. 'Selena blames Brian.'

'Not any more she doesn't! At least, not aloud,' he advised in a grim voice.

'You said something to her?' she hazarded. Perhaps Mrs Hirst's wish had come true, after all!

'Hmm . . .' His eyes lifted skywards as if he was mentally weighing whether he had or not. 'Mmm, I guess you could say that,' he said finally. 'Someone needed to. She would have spoiled everyone's afternoon otherwise.'

Kylie began fiddling with the handle of her racquet. 'She challenged me to a singles match,' she said, grimacing at the recollection.

'Then more fool her,' drawled Race, his lips curving in lazy amusement.

Glancing at him measuringly, she was silent for a moment, but suddenly it was impossible to keep the laughter from dancing into her eyes any longer. 'Would it be terribly conceited of me if I said that's what I thought?' she grinned irrepressibly.

His reciprocating laughter had her staring at him achingly. Oh, God, he could play havoc with her emotions so effortlessly at times!

'No, I'd say it was closer to terribly honest,' he smiled with heart-stopping attraction. 'Anyone with half an eye could see she'd be no match for you, tiger eyes. In singles, she needs more than just power to beat someone of your speed and ability.'

'I wonder if she will manage to arrange a match for us this afternoon, though,' she pondered speculatively. 'She said she intended to.'

Race gave a decidedly negative shake of his head. 'No, she was firmly outvoted by the rest of the Committee on that idea when she tried laying down the law to them back there,' nodding towards the homestead. 'If she wants to challenge you, it will have to be on some other day. There wouldn't be time to fit in another match this afternoon, and the Committee didn't think it fair that others should miss out on a game just because Selena felt she needed to prove something.' His expression turned wryly quizzical. 'Are you disappointed?'

'Not really,' she smiled. 'From what I've seen and heard so far, either way—if she wins, or loses—Selena's likely to be unbearable. So I'd much rather let the whole thing die a natural death, if possible. Besides, I don't like grudge matches, I prefer to enjoy my tennis.'

'Well, you certainly make it enjoyable to watch. That last drop volley of yours was as pretty as you'll ever see anywhere.'

'Thank you.' She dipped her head unassumingly. 'Although I think I was just lucky it came off as well as it did. It's not always one of my most reliable shots, and I have been known to massacre them before today.' Her lips twitched humorously in remembrance.

'Selena and Brian are probably wishing you had this afternoon too,' he said drily. 'You do realise it was you who made every one of your and Adrian's points in that tie-breaker, don't you?'

'No, I didn't actually,' she half laughed, surprise foremost. 'All I can remember is panicking at the thought of them being four points ahead.'

'Then you must panic very calmly, because it certainly didn't show,' Race drawled, and lithely eased himself upright as someone called to him from a group some distance away.

'Maybe not outside, but inside it's a different story,' she relayed. The same as now, she added to herself ruefully, as I pretend it doesn't matter to me whether you join those people over there, when really I don't want you to leave at all.

The man called to Race again, accompanying it with a beckoning arm this time, and burying her own wishes Kylie made herself smile lightly upwards.

'You'd better go, he's getting anxious.'

'Mmm, so it would appear,' he granted readily, but still making no move to accede to the man's invitation. 'But then that's nothing unusual for Lewis. Have you met him yet?'

She moved her head slightly, negatively. 'No, I don't think so.'

'Then I suppose we'd better rectify the omission, hadn't we?' Race smiled, holding out a hand to her. 'That is, if you would like to meet them.' He indicated the group as a whole.

'Oh, yes, I'd like that very much,' Kylie told him shyly, and struggling hard not to allow her pleasure at his suggestion show too much as she gained her feet and laid her racquet down on the bench. With him being so engagingly amenable, just the knowledge that he apparently wasn't in any rush to be rid of her company was enough to evoke an emotional high on her part, and she moved around the seat to join him with an elated spring in her steps.

CHAPTER EIGHT

In the days that followed as Kylie more often than not now that the shearing was under way drove Race over to the woolshed, which was sited on the boundary between Wanbanalong and Elouera Springs for convenience, and continued to give her assistance in other ways—though to a lesser degree as each succeeding week passed—she found it becoming harder and harder to keep her feelings under control where he was concerned.

His attitude had changed completely from what it had been in the beginning, and although he had never again made any attempt to kiss her since the night she had lost her way—much to her chagrin, at times—he still retained those disturbing habits of curling his fingers within her hair and smoothing his fingers gently up and down her neck whenever she was close to him. On a couple of occasions she had turned and found him watching her with a certain look in those beautiful green eyes of his which was capable of making her go weak at the knees, but as he always continued with whatever he was doing as if nothing out of the ordinary had taken place, she began to suspect it was a trick of the light or her own wishful thinking working overtime.

There were no doubts in her mind regarding how the thought of leaving with Grant when the time came affected her, however, for as each day brought their departure date nearer she was aware of a growing despondency at the idea of her probably never seeing Race again. And so it was that she awoke with mixed feelings on the appointed day for his return to the hospital and the removal of his cast and supporting bandages. On the one hand she was looking forward to seeing him without their encumbrance, but on the other, once he had no need of them any more then he would also have no need for her and Grant's assistance either, and consequently, there would be nothing to keep them from resuming their travels.

Dressed in a navy blue skirt, with a white knitted cotton tube top which left her smooth shoulders bare, Kylie returned to her room after breakfast that morning to collect a white shoulder bag from her dresser before taking one last cursory look in the mirror and heading for the front verandah.

Race and Grant were talking near the steps when she arrived and her employer watched her approach with a smile.

'Your last morning as chauffeuse on Wanbanalong, eh, little one?' he remarked jovially, and totally unaware of the sharp stab of pain his words caused.

'I guess so,' she shrugged as naturally as possible.

'And you'll be glad to be back to managing everything for yourself, I suppose?' It was to his nephew that he addressed that laughing comment.

'It has its compensations,' Race allowed wryly. 'Not that I would wish to appear ungrateful for all the help you've both given me, of course, but . . .'

'I know, I know.' Grant slapped him understandingly on the shoulder before taking a few steps in the direction of the door. 'I was just as independent as you are when I was your age. Only these days,' his eyes slanted wickedly, 'I'm old enough to enjoy having everything done for me by a pretty young girl.'

Despite herself, Kylie had to laugh, the smile lingering softly on her lips as she watched his departing figure fondly.

'You think a lot of him, don't you?' Race's voice cut in on her reverie.

She nodded silently, her thought processes still continuing. There must have been something about the Brandon males that struck a responsive chord deep within her, she reflected pensively, because in differing ways she loved them both. Abruptly she caught her breath in her throat as the import of her involuntary admission sank in, and her eyes flashed nervously to Race, fearful that she might have communicated her realisation to him in some way.

Fortunately for her, he had also been watching his uncle—thereby missing her anxious glance—and by the time he turned back to her she had her expression carefully controlled.

'It's getting late, we'd better be going,' she said briskly in an effort to forestall him continuing the conversation, and started down the steps towards the waiting station wagon.

Race grimaced somewhat sardonically at her officious tone but didn't comment until they were both seated in the vehicle and Kylie had it moving. Then he quizzed in dry accents, 'So what's bitten you this morning?'

Deliberately refusing to look at him, she hunched a dispassionate shoulder. 'Nothing that I know of.'

'No?' His mouth crooked lazily as he settled his muscled length more comfortably on the seat, the brim of his ever-present bush hat tilting slightly over his fore-head and giving him a tantalisingly rakish air. 'You're as quiet as a church mouse at breakfast; you come out-side looking as joyful as you would at a funeral; and then you suddenly become all very efficient and work-manlike.' From the corner of his eye he directed her an all too knowing glance. 'You surely don't still expect me to believe *something* isn't sadly awry, do you?' he mocked.

'That's up to you, of course.'

'Kylie!' he cautioned softly.

'Well, what do you want me to say?' she demanded fractiously, dismayed to find a suspicious dampness beginning to well into her eyes. 'Okay, so I'm not the life and soul of the party! Maybe I'm worried about your visit to the hospital today.'

'And maybe you're lying,' his voice roughened mini-mally.

'Thanks! It's always nice to be told your concern isn't appreciated.'

'Oh, come off it, sweetheart! Just what do you take me for?' he snapped sceptically, his rugged form tauten-ing with the first signs of anger. 'You're as aware as I damned well am that there's no need for any concern. These breaks haven't given me any trouble for some time now, and you know it! In truth, for the last couple of weeks I could just as easily have ridden down to the woolshed, instead of being driven by you!'

'So why didn't you?' she flared, angry at herself for having purposely said all the wrong things, but irra-tionally wanting to vent her annoyance on him for not having accepted them.

'I'm beginning to wonder!'

The dampness in Kylie's eyes became a definite veil of water which she had to blink away in order to continue driving. Now what had she done? She had completely ruined the accord which had been built between them during the last few weeks so that they had turned a full circle to bring them back to square one. And all because she had just realised she'd fallen hopelessly in love with him!

It wasn't his fault she couldn't control her foolishly wayward emotions, she berated herself inwardly. She should have known better than to have allowed them to become so involved, and especially since she had known right from the beginning just what his thoughts were regarding women. But to have started an argument in order to defend her feelings, that was the worst stupidity of all, she went on scathingly. Now she had probably destroyed whatever chance she might have had of at least gaining some enjoyment from his company during the days that were left to her.

With a sigh she sent him a covert sidelong glance, but seeing the tense set of his features she swung her eyes back to the road again in despair. She would have liked to have offered an apology of some kind, but with him looking so forbidding it was hard to find the right words to start, and as kilometre followed upon kilometre it became even harder, until at last they reached the city outskirts and still there hadn't been a word said by either of them to break the strained silence.

As she pulled up outside the hospital Kylie knew she couldn't let him go inside without wishing him well in some form or another, and she half turned in her seat to do so.

Before she could say a word, Race opened the door

and alighted, swinging it shut again, and then barely lowering his head to advise through the window, 'Park anywhere. I'll find it.'

Unwittingly denying her the opportunity to voice the solicitous phrases trembling on her lips, he spun on his heel and covered the distance between the car and the hospital doors with long purposeful strides.

Kylie didn't take her eyes off him until he had disappeared inside the building—just in case he turned back for a moment—but when he didn't, she uttered a half choked sob of anguish and the warm salty tears she had been holding at bay for so long at last began to stream down her cheeks.

It took her a while to find a parking space, but luckily she eventually located someone who was leaving and availed herself of theirs, a nice shaded alley which she drove into thankfully. It was too hot to be sitting in the sun for long, and she definitely didn't fancy waiting inside the hospital if there was any chance of someone noticing she'd been upset. That receptionist might just take it upon herself to phone through to Race's doctor again!

By watching through the rear vision mirror she was just able to see the hospital entrance, and when Race presently made his reappearance—his visit having taken nowhere near as long this time—she could study him unobserved as he scanned the parked vehicles searching for the station wagon.

Of their own volition her lips curved into a small pleased smile to see both his arms swinging free and easily by his sides as he walked towards the vehicle, although it had been replaced by an expression of extreme wariness by the time he made it to her door.

'I'll drive,' he stated brusquely, opening it.

With the merest of nods Kylie eased across to the passenger's side so he could slide in behind the wheel, and promptly felt her chin ensnared by fingers which forced her to look to the right as he pulled the door closed again.

'You've been crying,' he charged in slightly softer tones.

Kylie moved restlessly under his intent gaze. 'Mmm, silly of me, wasn't it?' It would have been pointless attempting to deny it. 'But don't let it bother you, I promise not to embarrass you by losing control while you're here.'

Race muttered something unintelligible beneath his breath and released her abruptly, devoting his attention to reversing the vehicle with fiercely controlled movements. Kylie slumped dejectedly against the seat. Just what the hell was she trying to do? Antagonise him to such an extent that he would never discover her true feelings because he wouldn't even be talking to her? Surely there was no need to go to those extremes!

They were out of the hospital grounds now and following a road she didn't recognise, but for the moment that was the least of her interests as she aimed a nervously apologetic glance in his direction.

'I'm sorry,' she offered in a small voice.

'For what?' he countered coldly, not even bothering to turn his head by so much as a centimetre. 'For being perverse . . . or typically feminine? Or maybe the two just automatically go hand in hand.' He laughed mirthlessly to himself.

The claim that she had been perverse she could understand, but . . . 'Typically feminine?' she sought enlightenment with a frown.

'Mmm, I've seen it all before,' he grimaced bitterly. 'It was a favourite trick of my mother's, to create an argument and then resort to tears in an effort to make my father believe he was the one in the wrong.' Now he looked at her, a brief but hard-eyed gaze of denunciation. 'Women! Every damned one of you is the same!'

'And men aren't, I suppose?' she gibed defensively. It hadn't been her intention at all to make him feel at fault for their argument.

'Quite possibly we are, but at least if we've got something to gripe about we come right out and say it! We don't get a fit of the sulks and refuse to discuss the matter!'

Kylie's indignation rose rapidly. 'I was not sulking!' she blazed. 'And—and I've already said I was sorry!'

'Which conveniently closes the chapter, is that it?' One well shaped brow lifted caustically.

'Well, I—I . . .' She spread her hands helplessly. 'What else do you expect me to say?'

'Right at present, I would suggest you don't say *anything*!' he returned, bitingly mocking. 'It appears to me that the more you say, the worse matters become.'

Truthfully, it wasn't an allegation she could gainsay, she realised dismally, and turned her attention to the passing scenery.

'Where are we going, anyway?' she asked indifferently a few minutes later. 'Or is this another route home?'

'No, it's not, but as I'd already planned on coming this way, I saw no reason to change my ideas just because you feel like being bloody difficult,' he goaded, but still managing to avoid telling her exactly where they were headed all the same, she noted with some asperity.

She was determined not to ask again, though, and bided her time—albeit a trifle vexedly—as the kilometres flew past until she could tell their destination for herself. Her first inkling came in the form of the unexpected shine of water in the distance, and as they drew nearer it became obvious it wasn't just a small body of it which had caught her eye, but a great expanse which stretched so far into the heat haze that it was almost impossible to see the other side.

Suddenly she recalled a part of Race's conversation from the day he had taken her to Silverton and, forgetting her decision not to ask for any information again, she questioned curiously, 'Are these the Menindee Lakes you were telling me about? The ones that supply Broken Hill with its water?'

'Mmm,' was all he would condescend to admit initially, but then, with an impassive shrug of wide shoulders, he expelled a deep breath and relented a little more to add, 'That's Lake Menindee itself, the largest of them.'

That she could believe. It looked enormous! 'How many are there altogether?'

'Eight main ones, together with a collection of minor lakes, depressions, and connecting channels,' he delivered in clipped tones.

'Man-made?'

'The lakes? No.'

They travelled over what Kylie guessed was one of the connecting channels he had mentioned, her lips pressing together wryly. She supposed she could count herself fortunate that he was answering at all, but at the

same time she did wish he would be a little more generous with his information.

'You mean, then, they've always been here but just
haven't been utilised before?' she probed a little further.

'Not really,' he shook his head, aggravatingly unco-
operative, and had her staring at him with ill-concealed
frustration.

She tried another approach. 'What made you come
out here today, Race? Business?' She was starting to
have suspicions of her own in that regard and wondered
if he would confirm them, or if she was barking up the
wrong tree entirely.

'Does it matter?' his counter-question came sardonically.

'Well, yes, I think so,' she persisted, undeterred.

'Why?'

Damn him! Did he always have to get the upper hand
when she needed it most? Now what did she say? That
she thought it might have been on her behalf he had
driven out there, and thereby give him the opportunity
to embarrass her by saying he had come on business, or
to visit friends? No way! she vowed mutely.

Turning off the highway on to a side road, Race
slanted her a goading look. 'Not so sure about that
now, huh?'

It was all Kylie could do to stop herself from slapping him. He knew! Without a doubt he knew what
she'd been thinking, and the unfeeling brute was ruth-
less enough to taunt her with the knowledge! She concentrated her gaze on her clenched hands, her dark hair
falling forward to brush silkily against her colouring
cheeks.

'That's right,' she finally concurred in a subdued and

throaty whisper. 'I've suddenly realised you were correct the first time . . . it *doesn't* matter.'

They were approaching the shores of a much smaller lake now and, following a sandy track around its grassy, tree-lined edge for some way, Race brought the station wagon to a halt beneath the shelter afforded by a stand of casuarinas.

Kylie was still sitting with her head downbent, and although she heard him toss his hat into the back and then the sound of his door opening, she didn't look up. That was, not until he stifled an exasperated oath and declared in the driest of accents, 'You may as well have a look now that we've stopped. You already know damned well you're the reason we came in the first place!'

So she had been right, after all. 'Then—then why did you . . .'

'Why not?' he cut in, his mouth shaping wryly, disarmingly, and obviously knowing exactly what she was going to ask. 'Maybe I considered a little retaliation was in order for what you've put me through this morning.' He began moving around to her side of the vehicle.

'I did say I was sorry for that,' she reminded him quietly, gaining her feet after he had opened her door.

'I know,' he sighed heavily, looking out over the lake, hands resting on lean hips. 'But that was after you'd made me feel a rotten swine for having made you cry.' He inclined his head ruefully to one side. 'I didn't like the feeling one little bit.'

'I'm sorry,' she apologised softly. 'Although that wasn't my intention, you know. To make you feel badly, or—or at fault.' Halting momentarily, sought his eyes shyly. 'I was just upset that we'd argued, and that you hadn't given me time to wish you luck before you went in to the hospital.'

'Oh, hell!' Race shook his head, rubbing a hand around his neck. He sank down agilely to sit with his back to one of the trees, forearms leaning on updrawn knees. 'Come here, tiger eyes,' he commanded lazily, indicating the grassy space beside him, and with an expression on his face she couldn't quite define.

There was no thought of refusal in Kylie's mind as she did as he suggested, even though her heart was hammering frantically at her ribs in response to the darkening look in his eyes, and once seated with her legs drawn close to her side she waited to hear what he had to say with a kind of breathless expectancy.

She didn't have long to wait, for Race promptly draped an arm across her shoulders, easing her closer, while his other hand cupped her face gently and tipped it up to his. 'I wonder if you have any idea just how much I've wanted to be able to hold you with two arms,' he murmured thickly against her willingly parting lips.

For once Kylie didn't attempt to pull away, but wound slim arms about his neck and answered with touchingly demure honesty, 'I hope it was as much as I've wanted to be held by them.'

With that fervent confession out in the open neither of them was interested in speaking any more, only in the feel of possessive lips being met by softly eager ones, and of strong arms moulding a warmly pliant figure to a hard sinewed length.

Swept along on a tide of consuming passion, Kylie didn't care whether Race guessed how deeply her emotions were involved or not. She was only living for the moment and the intoxicating rapture of knowing that she could arouse him to the same fever pitch as he did her.

Uttering a ragged groan, Race pulled her down lengthwise beside him, his long legs entangling with hers, and when his hands smoothed caressingly over the bare skin of her back she was unable to fight off any longer the ungovernable desire to touch his firm flesh too, and unfastening the buttons of his shirt she ran exploring fingers over the muscled ridges of his chest and shoulders beneath.

Leaning over her, he traced an erotic path from her lips to her ears, her throat, and the rising swell of her breasts above her strapless top with a warm mouth which sent shivers of ecstasy rippling throughout her curving form. And when a broad hand pushed the covering material of her top aside in order to cup one of those full, rosy-peaked mounds she arched convulsively closer to his powerful frame, and her lips began to savour the bronzed skin her fingers had bared.

It was Race who shuddered this time, his breath coming rapidly and erratically as he twined his fingers within her hair to draw her away from him. 'For God's sake, Kylie, don't make it any harder on me!' he pleaded in a voice made husky with strain and an undiminished desire. 'I already want you more than I ever believed it was possible to want anyone in my life!'

Shaken by the force of feelings which had prompted her to respond to his caresses so uninhibitedly, Kylie couldn't hold his smouldering gaze and lowered her thick lashes so that they lay like dark smudges against her cheeks. 'I'm sorry,' she breathed jerkily. 'But—but you shouldn't have . . .'

'Oh, sweetheart, I'm not complaining,' he interrupted heavily, cradling her head in the hollow of his shoulder. 'I'd like nothing more than for you to continue, and for our lovemaking to progress to its most natural and fulfilling conclusion. But not today, not like this, in the heat of the moment.' He tilted her face up to his with an inexorable forefinger. 'Marry me, Kylie!' he exhorted urgently. 'I haven't been able to get you out of my mind since the day I first met you, and I don't think I could bear the thought of a life without you in it now.'

Marry him! Joy burst through her system like the sun dispensing golden rays of warmth, even as her eyes began to fill with tears. 'Oh, yes!' she choked, half laughing, half crying. 'Although I never thought to hear you ask me that. You'd always made it so plain marriage wasn't for you.'

'Until a tiger-eyed slip of a girl made me realise just what I was missing,' he told her wryly. 'Of late, my most coveted aspiration has been to shackle you to my side for the rest of my life.'

'You really mean that?' She searched his face dazedly. It was all so completely unexpected!

'I do!' Abruptly, he gave a rueful laugh, shaking his head in disbelief. 'You've got me sounding as if I'm in church already.'

'I wish we were,' she sighed achingly. 'I love you so much I'm not sure I'll survive the waiting.' Her hands slid within the opened front of his shirt and she shyly smoothed them upwards until they came to rest on broad, firm shoulders. 'Ever since that afternoon at Elouera Springs—and perhaps even before—I think I've subconsciously been wanting you to make love to me.'

Race's arms tightened about her expressively. 'No more than I did, believe me!'

'Yet you haven't even made an attempt to kiss me for ages,' she accused with a provocative pout.

'Uh-uh,' he drawled laconically. 'I'd already found holding you with only one arm was too damned frustrating for words. I made myself a promise after that last time that I wouldn't be doing it again until I could do it thoroughly ... with the help of *both* arms.' His lips assumed a fascinatingly rueful curve. 'But as you can tell, I didn't intend waiting long once I did have the full use of the two of them again.'

Kylie's fingers linked about his neck to begin tugging his head down to hers. 'You do seem to be taking an uncommonly long time before repeating the procedure, though,' she teased, an eloquent glow in her eyes.

With a deeply stirring laugh, Race rolled on to his back, his securing arm pulling her on top of him. 'Not any longer, I'm not,' he assured her in impassioned tones and, with a hand on either side of her head, made certain he was as good as his word.

In the position she now found herself Kylie was more physically aware of him than she had ever been before and, as a result, her already heightened senses blazed into a new and uncontrollable life of their own, causing her to move against him restively, unwittingly sensuous.

Now she was all too conscious of her still naked breasts as they pressed against the light covering of hair on his chest, creating turbulent sensations she had never previously experienced, and sending her bloodstream racing. She ached with a desire she knew she couldn't control, wanting Race to assuage her need in the most satisfying way possible—by his complete and irrevocable possession of her body as well as her spirit—and so taken by surprise when he suddenly released her that she sagged weakly against him, her limbs feeling limp and powerless.

For a moment neither of them spoke as they allowed their breathing time to normalise, and then Kylie stirred slightly, her fingertips playing idly over the taut muscles in his upper arm.

'If you hadn't stopped, I wouldn't have been able to,' she confessed quietly.

In a supple movement Race swung her gently on to her back, and bending over her, planted a leisurely kiss on her receptive lips. 'I know,' he smiled tenderly.

'Oh! You mean, that's why—why you . . .' She pushed herself up into a sitting position, adjusting her cotton top feverishly, her cheeks staining with bright colour as she averted her gaze in embarrassment. 'I'm sorry. You must think I'm very lacking in . . .'

'Kylie, stop it!' he ordered roughly, and spun her back to face him with a hand gripping each of her shoulders tightly. 'Stop keep apologising all the time, and stop keep believing the worst of everything I say! I don't happen to think you're lacking in anything . . . save, perhaps, experience in this kind of situation.' His eyes softened unbelievably as he smiled down at her still worried features. 'Don't ever hide that loving nature of yours, sweetheart, it's one of your most endearing qualities.'

'You didn't seem to think so a moment ago,' she pointed out, grimacing dolefully.

'Not much I didn't!' The depth of feeling in his voice leaving her in no doubts in that regard. 'You'll never know what it cost me to call a halt when I did! But,' his lips twisted into a wry grin, 'not because I wanted to, believe me.'

'Then why?'

His grip on her shoulders loosened as his hands shifted inwards, his thumbs rubbing lightly against each side of her neck. 'Because I didn't want you to have any regrets afterwards. And there was a chance you might have had.'

'I doubt it,' she murmured honestly, albeit a little bashfully, and not quite able to hold his intense gaze. 'I—I don't think I've ever experienced quite so much pleasure as when you hold me and—and touch me.' Her eyes flickered upwards, but only so far as his throat as she put out a tentative hand to rest it against his tanned chest. 'And I like touching you too.' Nervously, her eyes at last met his. 'Is that very terrible of me? And to admit such a thing?'

'Oh, sweetheart, how can you ever think it might be?' he groaned, pulling her closer with encircling arms. 'I want you to enjoy touching me, as much as I enjoy touching you. The pleasure that's derived from making love is supposed to be for two to share, you know, not just one.'

And with him it would be pleasurable, she knew that instinctively. Sighing with a new contentment, she finally relaxed against his side, the hand which was still pressed to his chest diverting her thoughts.

'Anyway, you really shouldn't have pulled me on top of you like you did it could have caused some damage,' she admonished. 'That supporting bandage has only been off your ribs for a couple of hours.'

His eyes filled with dry humour. 'It still would have been worth it, but . . . no sweat. They're as right as rain now, and probably have been for quite a while, I reckon.'

'Yet you still had me drive you everywhere as if they weren't.' She wasn't certain whether she ought to be pleased or vexed.

'Of course.' He sent her thoughts spinning with a thoroughly satisfying kiss. 'By then I'd found I'd become extremely attached to my thoughtful little nursemaid and I liked having her around,' he admitted.

'The same as I wasn't averse to being with you either,' she dimpled radiantly. Her expression sobered slightly and she went on, 'That's partly why I—why I wasn't exactly a bundle of joy this morning. I wanted to see you without your bandages—just to see if you appealed as much without them as you did with,' she wrinkled her nose at him impudently, 'and yet I knew once you had them off you wouldn't need me around any more.'

'The hell I wouldn't!' he disagreed vibrantly. 'I trust you know differently from that now?'

'Mmm, I think I'm beginning to get the message,' she smiled winsomely.

The answering look in his eyes set her insides on fire. 'And the rest? he wanted to know. 'You said that was "partly" the reason.'

'Yes, well . . .' She trailed a forefinger absently down the firm skin inside his opened shirt. But only until she found her wrist imprisoned in a strong grasp which very definitely removed it from the vicinity.

'You keep doing that, and this conversation is going to have a very short life expectancy,' warned Race, drily mocking.

Kylie caught her bottom lip between pearly white teeth. 'Sorry,' she half laughed contritely. 'But to continue ... once again, as soon as those dressings were removed, then you wouldn't be needing Grant's and my assistance any longer. Which, of course, meant there would be nothing to stop us from setting off again.' Her lips curved into a faint smile, and she exhaled a heavy breath. 'And I just couldn't bear the thought of leaving.'

A sentiment he rewarded with an ardent possession of her more than willing lips before divulging, 'Thereby giving me one of the most confounding experiences of my life! I didn't know what the blazes to make of the way you were behaving, and when you wouldn't even discuss it . . .'

'How could I? I'd just realised I was in love with you.'

'That's no excuse,' he retorted in mock reproval, although his eyes said otherwise. 'Nor does it alter the fact that I still felt like wringing your neck for what you were putting me through.'

'And now?' she invited teasingly.

'You *know* what I want to do to you now, tiger eyes, so don't tempt me!'

'Promises, promises!' she dared to taunt with a laugh, then gave a squeal of part surprise, part apprehension, when he scooped her off the ground and into his arms as he rose fluidly upright.

'Mind your arm!' she gasped in consternation, her first thoughts for him even now.

'Well now,' he drawled lazily, his steps taking them closer to the lake, 'how does a cold bath appeal?'

Kylie clutched him around the neck in panic. 'You wouldn't!'

His only acknowledgment was to crook one dark brow in a challenging gesture and continue on to the edge of the water.

'*Race!*' she cried imploringly as she felt his hold starting to relax. 'Please! I'm sorry!'

With a broadening grin he caught her firmly back to his chest again and dropped a feather-light kiss on the tip of her nose. 'You were right the first time ... I wouldn't,' he disclosed gruffly. 'However ...'

'Mmm?' she smiled adoringly, her previous agitation forgotten.

'I think it will be easier for me to keep my hands off you, and therefore be less of a strain on my self-control, if we leave this rather idyllic spot, and ...'

'Visit the rest of the lakes?' she broke in quickly.

'You want to?'

'Please!'

His ensuing smile had her catching her breath in her throat. 'How can I refuse?'

'And you'll try to be a little more informative this time?' Kylie cajoled unashamedly.

'That too,' he acceded with an indulgent laugh.

'Starting where we left off, and explaining just how they did get there?' she suggested wryly.

'Okay, okay,' he laughed again. 'They used to be dry lakes which only filled in time of flood, but with a weir on the river and a regulator controlling Lakes Menindee and Cawndilla, the water doesn't go to waste any more.'

'Thank you,' she smiled for at last having been given her answer.

Race began heading for the station wagon, still carrying her, and clearly in no hurry to let her go. 'Anything else you want to know?' he drawled.

'Ah, well, now that you mention it . . .,' she began mischievously.

CHAPTER NINE

'WHAT do you think Grant will say?' Kylie asked as she walked through the sitting room with Race on their way to the office later that day.

'Probably nothing complimentary. At least, not to me, at any rate,' he smiled drily.

'Oh?' she puzzled. 'Why's that?'

He laid an arm comfortably about her shoulders, his head lowering conspiratorially. 'Because I'm about to deprive him of his most delightful travelling companion, and that he isn't going to appreciate in the slightest, I'm sure,' he advised with a totally unregretful grin.

Some of Kylie's happiness subsided a little. 'Yes, well, I do feel rather guilty about leaving him in the lurch.'

'There's no need,' he shrugged impassively. 'I should imagine he'll be able to find a replacement readily enough. In fact . . .' He stopped short, his mouth curving ironically, then gave a dismissive shake of his head.

The action brought a crease of puzzlement to Kylie's forehead and a look of uncertainty to her eyes. 'Yes . . .?' she prompted hesitantly.

'Later,' he negligently brushed her query aside.

'Why not now?' she pressed, a hint of wariness creeping in with the uncertainty.

He nodded to indicate the office doorway just ahead of them. 'No time,' he half laughed, and she, perforce, had to leave it at that.

Grant, as anticipated, was working at the desk inside the room, and his reaction to the news they had to impart was a threefold one. Surprise, that he had no clue as to what was taking place—as he put it—under his very nose. Pleasure, that his nephew had at last decided to surrender his single status—one crusty old bachelor was enough for any family, he declared—and for someone of whom he thoroughly approved. And lastly, though no less sincerely, disappointment that Kylie's days in his employ were numbered.

'Just considered your own wishes, did you?' he growled at Race in feigned disgust. 'With never a thought for how I might feel at having my companion ruthlessly plucked from me in mid-journey, as it were.'

'Well, as a matter of fact . . .,' Race began in a slow drawl, linking his hands behind his head as he leant back in his chair and surveyed his uncle banteringly across the desk. 'In that regard, you may be pleased to learn I haven't been letting the grass grow under my feet either.'

'Oh?' Both Kylie's and Grant's brows peaked in unison.

'Mmm,' he smiled complacently. 'I knew you wouldn't be relinquishing Kylie willingly, so I thought I'd lessen the blow a little by arranging for an eminently worthy successor to be all ready and waiting. Someone you already know and get along with very well.'

Grant started to laugh, knowing his nephew's organising abilities. 'And just who is this paragon?' he enquired, amused.

'Young Ivan Morphett.'

Male, of course! noted Kylie a little caustically,

unable to control her feeling of resentment at knowing Race had arranged this behind her back—and before she had even agreed to marry him! Nor did Grant's apparently more than delighted acceptance of the idea make her feel any better, and she listened to the rest of their conversation moodily.

'It's all arranged, you say?' Grant mused consideringly after his nephew had helpfully listed all the advantages of such an association.

Race flexed his shoulders and made a swaying gesture with one hand. 'As good as,' he verified laconically. 'All you need do is confirm it, and you'll be all set to go again. Although I wouldn't leave it too long before doing so, if I were you,' he added on a cautioning note, 'as Ivan was only saying the last time I spoke to him, if this doesn't come off, then he has something else in mind to try before finally deciding if he wants to settle down on the land or not.'

'In that case, perhaps I'd better get in touch with him as soon as possible. I might even drive over and see him this afternoon, in fact.' Grant rose decisively to his feet, reaching for the wide-brimmed hat which was hanging on a wall hook behind the desk. 'There's no time like the present, they say, and while the mood's upon me . . .' He stopped at the door to include them both in his smile, 'I'll see you later. And with good news, I trust.'

Silently Kylie accompanied Race to the back verandah, seeing Grant climb into the four-wheel-drive which had been parked outside, and giving a somewhat wistful acknowledging wave as the vehicle began to move. Immediately she turned to the man beside her and discovered him to have an altogether too satisfied look on his face for her liking right at present.

'You never did like the idea of me being his companion, did you?' she charged tautly.

'No, not particularly.' His return was candidly voiced.

She raised her chin challengingly higher, as much in an effort to stop its betraying tremble as anything. 'And right from my first night here you made it plain you thought Grant should have a male companion instead.'

'So? I still think it's preferable,' he half smiled.

'Even to the extent of arranging a substitute before he was aware he might need one?' Her voice rose a fraction.

'The opportunity was there, so I took it,' he advised, eyes narrowing slightly at the change in her tone.

'And you always get what you want?'

'If possible,' he conceded shortly.

Her breast rose and fell sharply in time with her rapid breathing. 'No matter what lengths you have to go to, and by whatever means are at your disposal ... right?'

'If that's what's needed, yes!' he agreed tersely. His annoyance was beginning to increase now too.

'Including devious means, Race?' she sniped, hands clenching convulsively at her sides. 'I believe that *was* the expression you used at the time, wasn't it?'

'No, if I remember correctly, that was the term *you* used!' he countered sarcastically, and then dragged an irritable hand through his hair. 'Although I wish to hell I knew just what you were getting at!'

Oh, yes, it would serve his ends to play innocent! Kylie heaved bitterly. But there had been something worrying at the back of her mind ever since their interlude by the lake that morning, and its cause had eluded

her until a few seconds ago. However, now that she
knew just what it was that had been pricking at her
subconscious, and taking into account his premeditated
sounding out of Ivan Morphett for her job, it only
made her more certain than ever that there could have
been more to his proposal of marriage than met the eye.

'I'll tell you what I'm getting at!' she returned bitterly, painfully, and struggling desperately to hold de-
solating tears in check. 'An offer of marriage which was
a sure-fire way of getting me out of Grant's employ,
that's what I'm talking about! One which could easily
have a stop put to it with a convenient argument and a
parting of the ways . . . *after* Grant had employed a
companion of whom you approved!' She took a deep
shuddering breath before rushing on, 'And you really
had me believing it for a while. It's amazing how we can
convince ourselves when we want to be convinced, isn't
it?' Her eyes widened in despairing self-mockery. 'The
only trouble was . . .'

'Kylie! Don't do this to . . .'

'You made one vital mistake, Race,' she continued as
if he hadn't interrupted. As if, having started, she
couldn't stop until she had said it all. 'You left out the
most important part of all! You forgot to say, "I love
you"!' she sobbed on an agonised note.

'For God's sake, Kylie!' Race stepped towards her
urgently.

'What, no hasty inclusion of those three comforting
words?' she taunted facetiously, her eyes misting un-
governably as she backed out of his reach. 'Well, never
mind, I didn't really expect there to be. You can't
say them because it wouldn't be true, would it?' she
cried brokenly, and spinning about, flew down the

steps on to the driveway.

'Kylie!'

She heard him roar her name behind her, but although there seemed a thread of warning in his call, she didn't stop running. At least, not until she heard a screech of brakes as Adrian came round the corner of the homestead in a Land Rover, but by then it was too late, and the two of them collided with a force which sent a stabbing pain through her side and had her losing consciousness before she even hit the ground.

When next she opened her eyes, Kylie felt as if her whole body was one huge, throbbing ache, and she swallowed automatically to relieve the dryness in her throat as she tried to gather her thoughts.

'So you're awake,' came a deep voice from somewhere beside her. 'How do you feel?'

Turning her head, she groaned—even that hurt—and discovered herself to be lying on her bed and Race occupying a chair close to her left side. Suddenly their last conversation flashed into her mind and she closed her eyes again defeatedly.

'Leave me alone,' she pleaded tearfully. Then, with tawny eyes staring at him bitterly, 'Haven't you done enough already?'

'Oh, Kylie!' He shook his head tiredly, and as the filtered light from the window glanced across his face she noticed the signs of strain about his finely sculptured mouth. 'You can't honestly believe I was faking the emotions I felt for you at the lake today?'

'Oh, no, you made it perfectly clear you *wanted* me, but that isn't quite the same, is it?' Her voice trembled traitorously and she turned her face away from him in order to hide her moistening lashes. 'Anyway, it's over. I don't want to talk about it any more.' She put a hand to her head as a wave of nausea washed over her and winced when her fingers came in contact with an extremely tender lump at her hairline. 'And—and I feel sick,' she murmured plaintively.

Race brushed her tousled hair back from her damp face in a compassionate gesture. 'I'm not surprised, that was a hell of a knock you took,' he said heavily. 'But I'm sorry I can't give you anything for it, you could have a touch of concussion.'

'Oh!' Her eyelids started to droop and she blinked them furiously open again. 'It hurts when I breathe too, and my arm's sore,' she mentioned absently.

'Mmm, they seem to have taken the brunt of it,' he advised sympathetically. 'But don't worry, the doctor's on his way, and once they get you into hospital they'll be able to replace the temporary measures we've applied and give you more comfort.'

'Hospital? Measures you've applied?' she echoed bewilderedly, and made to push herself up on her elbows to see for herself what he was talking about. When her right side and arm protested violently at her movements, and an attack of giddiness overcame her, she slumped back on to her pillow with as a smothered moan.

Kylie guessed she must have blacked out again for a little, because the next thing she knew Race was standing beside the bed, hands thrust into the back pockets of his pants, and she was certain she hadn't seen him move.

'Are you leaving?' she asked blankly.

A muscle jerked spasmodically beside his mouth and

he seated himself on the side of the bed this time. 'No, we still have something to discuss ... remember?'

'I said I didn't want to talk about it any more,' she reminded him querulously. And seeking to change the subject she fingered the thin sleeveless blouse she was wearing and queried, 'Why have I got this on? I didn't have before, did I?'

'No, Abby and I got you into that after I strapped your ribs.'

That piece of information really dispelled any feelings of drowsiness and she moved her left hand experimentally over her midsection. 'You mean, I broke a rib?' she half gasped, half laughed mockingly, and then grimaced at the ensuing pain.

'Take it easy,' Race cautioned roughly, seeing her bit hard on her lip. 'By the feel of it, I'd say you've done at least two ... and your arm.'

'And my arm,' she repeated vaguely.

'That's why it's so sore.'

A look of pure irony crossed her features. 'Well, it appears I certainly did my best to emulate you. You're positive I haven't broken my collarbone as well?'

Race answered that with a slow negating shake of his head, the wry smile catching at his lips still possessing the power to destroy her equilibrium even after all that had happened. 'I don't think either of us realised quite how prophetic my words were going to be when I said our positions would be reversed in a month's time. So, do I now copy you, and act as *your* nursemaid until you've recovered?' he teased lightly.

'No!' Kylie shifted restively under his emerald

gaze. 'Seeing Grant no longer has any use for my services, I shall be going home as soon as I'm able to travel.'

'The hell you will!'

'You can't stop me!'

'Can't I?' Leaning forward, he supported his weight on one hand beside her shoulder, while his left forefinger sensuously traced the outline of her quivering lips. 'We'll see about that.'

'Oh, please!' Kylie closed her eyes in order to shut out his attractively wrought features. 'You've got what you wanted. I'm not Grant's companion any longer. What more do you want of me?'

A warm mouth replaced the finger against her lips, making her breath catch in her throat at the gentle, persuasive pressure he was exerting, and feebly trying to evade the caresses she so much desired.

'I want *you*, tiger eyes,' he declared huskily. 'Nothing else but you.'

'Physically, you mean?' She tried to keep her tone uncaring, but it just wasn't possible, and she knew her deep hurt showed.

'No, not just physically!' Race denied categorically. 'I want you mentally and spiritually as well! And why?' His mouth twisted sardonically. 'Because I damned well love you, that's why!' He bent to touch his lips to hers, repeating, 'I—love—you,' against their tremulous softness.

Golden-brown eyes flew to his feverishly. She was desperate to believe him, and yet . . . 'Why didn't you say so before, then? Why wait until now? Because you're feeling sorry for me?' she just had to question.

'Oh, sweetheart,' he groaned, shaking his head sadly.

'It has nothing to do with my feeling sorry for you, even though I do, and especially since it's my fault you were hurt. I would far rather have had it happen to me again than to you.' Easing away from her slightly, he rubbed his fingers across his forehead, expelling a long slow breath. 'Unfortunately, however, it wasn't until I saw you run into the path of the Land Rover that I could admit, even to myself, that I loved you. I was more than willing to give you my name, but my heart . . .' he smiled ruefully, 'well, that was something else again. The final barrier against total commitment to a member of the opposite sex, you might say. You see, I swore to myself years ago that I'd never give any woman the weapons to tear me apart like my mother did my father.' His expression hardened with remembrance. 'And all because he loved her!'

Tears gathered at the corners of Kylie's eyes and spilled on to creamy cheeks. 'Race, I'm so sorry,' she whispered abjectly.

'For what, tiger eyes?' he quizzed, bending over her, but carefully so as not to touch her injuries.

'For all the things I accused you of doing.'

'W-e-ll,' he drew the word out in a lazy drawl, 'I must admit there was some truth in part of it. I did approach Ivan about becoming Grant's companion/driver solely for the purpose of depriving you of the job.' He grinned with indolent devilry. 'Hell, I wanted you for myself, not traipsing around the country with my damned uncle. I had better things in mind for you to be doing.'

'Such as?' she ventured to ask with a smile on having her last doubts finally swept away.

'Oh, this and that,' he replied vaguely, although his

long electrifying capture of her lips wasn't indecisive at all.

With one good arm resting about his neck, Kylie eyed him persuasively. 'I don't really have to go to hospital, do I, Race? Couldn't the doctor just bandage me up here?'

''Fraid not, my love,' he disappointed her apologetically. 'Apart from that arm of yours needing more than just bandaging, all chest injuries have to X-rayed.'

'I won't have to be away long, though, will I?' she sighed. Every moment spent away from him would seem like an eternity now.

'Probably only overnight,' he smiled reassuringly. 'Unless, of course, that bump on your head makes them suggest otherwise. But I expect it will be okay for Grant to drive in and collect us in the morning.'

'Us?'

'Mmm, you didn't think I'd let you fly into town with the doctor all on your own, did you?' he grinned.

Kylie drew his head down to hers, cursing the injuries that prevented her from holding him as she would have liked, and attempting to convey the depth of her love with her lips alone.

'Eight weeks,' Race groaned hoarsely when at last they parted. 'I don't think I could possibly wait any longer.'

'For what?'

'Us to be married,' he told her deeply. 'And if it hadn't been for those,' wryly indicating her bandages, 'it could have been eight *days*!'

'Don't remind me,' she begged, her own disappointment all too plain to see.

Although, when she came to think of it—some enraptured moments later—perhaps eight weeks wasn't really such a long time. Not when there was a whole lifetime of loving ahead of them!

Harlequin Plus
A WORD ABOUT THE AUTHOR

As a child Kerry Allyne often occupied herself by spinning short stories, without ever actually imagining she might write anything for publication. But when her youngest child started school, Kerry took out her trusty typewriter and set about trying to fill in the days by writing a novel.

For inspiration she had only to look out her window over a garden filled with flowering frangipani, hibiscus and azalea. For a title she had only to think about Australia's wet season (summer), which brings lovely compensation in the form of a dozen kinds of tropical fruits. And so *Summer Rainfall* was born, published by Harlequin as Romance #2019 in 1976.

Kerry and her husband run a small electrical-contracting business, and when she isn't writing novels she keeps the company's accounts. When she isn't doing that she helps care for the small herd of cattle and assorted hens that share her acreage.

She and her husband enjoy fishing as a hobby. Another interest is genealogy, largely because her husband's ancestors were among the very earliest settlers to Australia.

Kerry, on the other hand, is a more recent settler; she was born in England and as child emigrated with her family. Despite her relative newcomer status—or quite possibly because of it—Kerry Allyne writes of Australia and its people with authenticity and love. And it is this spirit of enthusiasm and romace that has won her the loyalty of millions of readers all over the world.

FREE!

A hardcover Romance Treasury volume
containing 3 treasured works of romance
by 3 outstanding Harlequin authors...

...as your introduction to Harlequin's
Romance Treasury subscription plan!

...almost 600 pages of exciting romance reading
every month at the low cost of $6.97 a volume!

A wonderful way to collect many of Harlequin's most beautiful love
stories, all originally published in the late '60s and early '70s.
Each value-packed volume, bound in a distinctive gold-embossed
leatherette case and wrapped in a colorfully illustrated dust jacket,
contains...
- 3 full-length novels by 3 world-famous authors of romance fiction
- a unique illustration for every novel
- the elegant touch of a delicate bound-in ribbon bookmark...
  and much, much more!

Romance Treasury

...for a library of romance you'll treasure forever!

Complete and mail today the FREE gift certificate and subscription
reservation on the following page.

Romance Treasury

An exciting opportunity to collect treasured works of romance! Almost 600 pages of exciting romance reading in each beautifully bound hardcover volume!

You may cancel your subscription whenever you wish! You don't have to buy any minimum number of volumes. Whenever you decide to stop your subscription just drop us a line and we'll cancel all further shipments.

FREE GIFT!
Certificate and Subscription Reservation

Mail this coupon today to
Harlequin Reader Service
In the U.S.A.
1440 South Priest Drive
Tempe, AZ 85281

In Canada
649 Ontario Street
Stratford, Ontario N5A 6W2

Please send me my FREE Romance Treasury volume. Also, reserve a subscription to the new Romance Treasury published every month. Each month I will receive a Romance Treasury volume at the low price of $6.97 plus 75¢ for postage and handling (total—$7.72). There are no hidden charges. I am free to cancel at any time, but if I do, my FREE Romance Treasury volume is mine to keep, without any obligation.

NAME _____
(Please Print)

ADDRESS _____

CITY _____

STATE/PROV. _____

ZIP/POSTAL CODE _____

Offer expires December 31, 1982
Offer not valid to present subscribers.   D2479